…NTENTS

…TIME

Nº 33

Publisher
Crime Time
7a King Henry's Walk
Islington
London N1 4NX
Fax: 020 7249 5940
e-mail: editor@crimetime.c…
Website: www.crimetime.co.uk

Distribution
Turnaround

Printing
Cox & Wyman

Editor
Barry Forshaw

Associate editor
Judith Gray

Production editor
Paul Brazier

Film editor
Michael Carlson

TV & music editor
Charles Waring

Regular contributors
Mike Ashley
Natasha Cooper
Mark Campbell
Maxim Jakubowski
Russell James
Kim Newman
Paul McAuley

Advertising
ads@crimetime.co.uk
Tel: 01582 761264

Subscriptions
See page 96
£20 for 4 issues (£30 outside UK)
to: Crime Time Subscriptions,
Oldcastle Books Ltd
P O Box 394
Harpenden, AL5 1XJ
www.crimetime.co.uk

 ISBN 1-84243-090-4

Articles

Regular Features

Columns

Reviews

Subscriptions & Special Offers

FROM THE DESK

Is there too much crime fiction being published? For those in the book trade who are not aficionados of the genre, the answer to that is unquestionably yes, with more and more authors chasing a beleaguered crime readership every month. Certainly, the offices of *Crime Time* receives a sackful of new hopefuls every morning. And how much of it is any good? SF writer Theodore Sturgeon once famously opined that "90% of everything is crap", and it's possible to argue that dictum certainly applies to the crime novel. But wasn't it ever thus? Looking back to both the golden age of the English detective story and the glorious era of the American pulps, it's easy to forget that many once-popular authors have (deservedly) fallen by the wayside; history has a way of sorting out those things that deserve a long shelf life. Actually, the key question is not whether or not too much has been published, but how one sifts through the mass of new releases to find worthwhile material. Hopefully, *CT* can fulfil that function to some degree, and as we try to focus mostly on those writers and books we like, you can (largely speaking) rest assured that inclusion in these pages guarantees a certain level of expertise and interest.

As yet, we have no feedback on our violence issue; this issue we're back to our author-focus theme: an in-depth study by our experts which (hopefully) provides the last word on Sue Grafton... for the time being, at least. In this issue you'll also find an exclusive extract from the new No Exit Press reissue of Georges Simenon's *Red Lights*; we're hoping this will whet your appetite for our forthcoming Simenon issue, which will be tied in to the major events in this Simenon Festival year.

Barry Forshaw

Our website (www.crimetime.co.uk) adds a selection of articles, news and reviews on a weekly basis, so finding that half-remembered piece on Dorothy Sayers or James M Cain might be a little easier online than thumbing through your yellowing issues of the magazine.

LOCATING SUE GRAFTON

Gill Plain

For the past ten years teaching and writing about crime fiction has been an integral part of my life – and yet for some reason Sue Grafton has never featured in this process. Instead she remains one of the few high profile crime writers whose books I have simply read. The 'alphabet' series has just been there, like Kinsey Millhone's duvet, a source of comfort reserved for rainy Sunday afternoons. So it was with some trepidation that I approached the process of casting a critical eye over Grafton's prolific output. With the series now standing at 17, a full scale survey seemed impossible, so I opted for the beginning and what might be termed the ending-to-date. Unfortunately it transpired that my copies of *A is for Alibi* and *B is for Burglar* had disappeared on 'loan perpetual', so by an admirably scientific process of elimination I arrived at a sample comprising *C is for Corpse* (1986), *O is for Outlaw* (1999) and *P is for Peril* (2001). As it turned out I had little reason to regret my choice – not least because the process of reading and re-reading left me with a sense of Grafton's novels and her heroine that did not quite fit the critical parame-

ters within which she has so far been discussed. The following, then, is an attempt to 'locate' Sue Grafton within the traditions of American crime writing.

A survey of the critical landscape reveals that Grafton has been acknowledged and applauded as one of a founding triumvirate of hardboiled women crime writers. In a recent study by Hans Bertens and Theo D'haen, she is described as having made a 'seminal' contribution to the genre, and along with Sara Paretsky and Marcia Muller, is awarded the perhaps somewhat dubious accolade of being dubbed a 'grand old lady'. Bertens and D'haen are obviously not the first to compare these writers. In 1994 Sally Munt identified Grafton and Paretsky as exemplary producers of 'liberal feminist' crime fiction – an appellation in Munt's book that is almost synonymous with the failure of political agency. But Munt's analysis

is useful, not least because it also provides a succinct account of what distinguishes these two writers. "Warshawski", she observes, "offers a fantasy of femininity, whereas Millhone offers relief from femininity." While a little harsh on Paretsky, this is an admirable description of Kinsey Millhone. Famously lacking any 'feminine' clothing beyond her all-purpose black dress, the early novels make comic play out of Kinsey's distance from 'appropriate' femininity. In *C is for Corpse*, for example, she makes a desperate attempt to conform for the benefit of her wealthy client's family, scrabbling around the back seat of her car to construct an outfit:

> On the floor, I found a pair of black spike heels I'd bought when I'd intended to pass myself off as a hooker in a tacky part of Los Angeles. When I'd gotten there, of course, I'd discovered that all the whores looked like college girls, so I'd abandoned the disguise.

Inevitably her impersonation of classy femininity is as inadequate as her attempt at its opposite, and the critics Priscilla Walton and Manina Jones have applauded Grafton's capacity to 'disrupt normative gender and sexual representation' through ironic commentary and comic spectacle. The conventions of femininity are a closed book to Millhone, and as the novels have progressed, Kinsey's 'failure' has ceased to become an object of self-conscious comedy, mutating instead into the blunt assertion of subjectivity found in *P is for Peril*:

> I felt less than glamorous in my jeans and turtleneck, but it couldn't be

helped. I didn't have time to go home and change. Into what? I don't have anything else. This is what I wear.

Later in the book this refusal of femininity is reinforced by Millhone's self-conscious description of herself as 'Philip Marlowe in drag'. Although initially the comparison seems misleading – drag implying a conscious deployment of femininity of which Millhone is constitutionally incapable – when considered in relation to the novel's narrative voice, the image becomes altogether more appropriate. I suggested above that Sally Munt, as a critic, is somewhat disappointed in the feminism of Grafton and Paretsky, describing the 'New Woman' detective as 'a sheep in wolves' clothing'. Scott Christianson, however, offers a rather different point of view. In an article exploring Grafton's use of the classic devices of hardboiled narrative – tough talk and wisecracks – Christianson suggests that: "Like her many male counterparts – Sam Spade, Philip Marlowe, Lew Archer, and Spenser – Millhone attempts to order her chaotic and violent experience in a careful narrative which, above all, tries to remain true to her experience even when she cannot make sense of what exactly is happening to her."

The crucial point about these novels as feminist texts, he concludes, is their appropriation of hardboiled language to inscribe a specifically female subjectivity. The Millhone books, he claims, "explore what it means to be a woman with the emphasis on *a* woman, who happens to be a hardboiled private detective". Christianson's perspective is shared by more recent commentators such as Bertens and D'haen, who see the significance of Millhone residing in her capacity to make us question both detective absolutes and the value of the patriarchal social structures that shape and constrain the lives of the women and men caught within them. Grafton, then, has succeeded where many have failed. She has constructed a female detective capable of inhabiting the form of hardboiled detection while yet problematising its prejudices and limitations. Yet for me, the picture that has emerged above does not quite capture the dominant tone or mood of the novels. Perhaps this is because I cannot seem to locate them comfortably within the hardboiled template. Christianson commends Millhone's use of 'language as power' – both in her public encounters with a frequently hostile world, and in her private accounting of events. Undoubtedly the interior world of the private investigator is convincingly

reshaped by Millhone's doubts, desires and contrary perspective, but the empowerment of the narrative voice must be set against the limitations of her public persona. Kinsey seems capable of wisecracking only when in disguise or under threat – when she is lying, assuming a false identity, or putting a brave face on the prospect of imminent death. When presenting herself without this shield, she appears more frequently paralysed than empowered by social discourse – especially when detached from her familiar blue-collar environment. Encounters with the idle rich prompted Philip Marlowe to some of his sharpest witticisms. In the same situation, Kinsey Millhone is, often as not, rendered speechless.

The public/private tension encapsulated here speaks to a fundamental conflict in the character Grafton has created. Kinsey Millhone is a woman forced prematurely into adulthood, who would, ideally, like nothing better than to retreat into childhood. The oft-repeated story of the death of her parents is central to the narrative. Abandoned at the age of five, and brought up by a kind but distant aunt, she seems to have bypassed the processes of play and companionship. In all its retellings, her narrative skips from the loss of her parents to the catastrophes of her marriages, pausing only occasionally to comment on the experiences of her lonely childhood (1986: 190-191). Not surprisingly, in adulthood she has emerged as a loner, but she cannot evade the pull of a past she was denied. This tension manifests itself in three key tropes: her pattern of living, her transgressive fantasies, and a process of unresolved mourning that shapes and constrains the choices she makes in her adult relationships. To expand: Kinsey lives in a doll's house under the kindly supervision of her fairy godfather, Henry Potts. She has, in effect, never left the single room of childhood, and her greatest comfort is to retreat to this space. In more recent novels her relationship to her room has changed. Initially the converted garage that is her apartment was excessively minimalist – an encampment that could be left at any minute, but since its refit in the style of a compact yacht, it has evolved into a fantastical bolt hole within which she can escape from the effort of public life. And encountering the world *is* an effort. The language of the novels constructs daily living through a series of verbs that exaggerate the actions involved. Kinsey 'snags' her drinks, 'hauls' out her typewriter, 'hefts' her bag. When she starts up her car she 'fires' up the engine and 'snaps' on the lights. While on one level the diction implies urgency and purpose, the cumulative effect is wearing. After a day spent toting, hefting and hauling, it is no surprise that Millhone finds exercise hard to contemplate.

The transgressive fantasies are perhaps less unusual. Behind a fairly placid exterior – unlike Warshawski, Millhone is slow to anger – Grafton's detective seethes with inappropriate, often violent urges. Confronted by an unwelcome figure from the past, a fantasy revenge erupts into her consciousness: "I wanted to lift her front chair legs and flip her backward, just for the satisfaction of hearing her head thud against the stone floor." These eruptions parallel the drives of early life, variously manifesting themselves as sexual desire, violence and a cheerful scatological fascination with what lies beneath: "Everything looked spotless. I wondered where the little birdies dropped their tiny green and white turds." Kinsey Millhone does not want to play with the grown-ups, and when she confronts the world as an adult, it is always with the eyes of the child looking out from within. Finally Millhone is locked into the past by the impossibility of completing a mourning process initiated by the death of her parents. The frequent repetition of this, her birth myth or origin story, bears witness to its fundamental importance in the shaping of the detective's character. Her losses as a child have left a legacy that manifests itself in a repeated attraction towards those in some way marked by loss or death. From Bobby Callahan, the initially disabled and soon to be dead client she is drawn to in *C is for Corpse* to the misfit brother Guy Malek in *M is for Malice*, Kinsey's choice of attachments indicate both a repeated reworking of the grief experience (as these characters typically die, exposing the detective afresh to the betrayal of bereavement) and a search for others as detached as she is from the comfortable conventions of society. In her attraction to those who have suffered, and who she recognises as being like her, Kinsey repeatedly risks further betrayal, and a perilous re-encounter with the pain she is seeking to assuage. Grafton makes the dilemma explicit at the end of *F is for Fugitive*, concluding Kinsey's narrative with an impossible question: "If love is what injures us, how can we heal?"

Re-reading, then, reminded me of the pervasive melancholy that underpins Millhone's character – a subdued self-containment that adds an air of disquiet to the character's otherwise convincing claim to take pleasure in her own company. And perhaps it is this trace of mourning that explains why the detective landscape of which I was most reminded in *P is for Peril* was the bleached and melancholic suburban California of Joseph Hansen's early Dave Brandstetter novels. Although the two detectives come from different ends of the social and sexual spectrum, they both shuttle in their mismatched cars between the empty palaces of the wealthy and the desolate spaces of the poor, exposing in the process the bleak disfunctionality at the heart of American life. Both Brandstetter and Millhone repeatedly uncover the failure of the American dream as manifested in the imperatives of heterosexual family life. Grafton's novels are peppered with disenchanted couples, bitter divorces, destructive family ties. In this context it is hardly surprising that Millhone feels little need to fight her inclination towards solitude. The family, Grafton tells us, is oppressive and potentially deadly – which perhaps accounts for Kinsey's reluctance to embrace the cousins who emerged mid-series as a curious throwback to her unresolved past. Indeed, anything that smacks of family distresses her, as is evident in *P is for Peril*, when Kinsey contemplates the drawbacks of renting space from Lonnie Kingman:

> Where once I'd been attracted to the sense of family I felt at the firm, now all I saw were attendant psychodramas. Jeniffer was Cinderella with a diminutive IQ. Ida Ruth and Jill, like the spiteful stepsisters, were simperingly nice to her in person but talked about her behind her back every chance they could. I'm not sure what part I played,

but I did my best to avoid participation by hiding in my room.

Hiding in the sanctuary of her room, the child Kinsey spies on the vagaries of the 'adult' world into which she was so precipitously thrust. Small wonder that as an adult herself she gives few hostages to a public sphere she recognises as fundamentally untrustworthy. In her undemonstrative way, then, Grafton has succeeded in satisfying both critical and popular taste, and has seen her consciously anti-feminine detective take up comfortable residence at the heart of a central American trope. But at some level I wonder whether Kinsey is not so much anti-feminine as pre-pubescent and, as she evades the imperatives of patriarchy behind her duvet and a good book, she reminds me above all of the child camping out in her parent's garden, playing with an independence that is as scary as it is liberating.

References

Contemporary American Crime Fiction
by Hans Bertens and Theo D'haen
(Palgrave, 2001)
Feminism in Women's Detective Fiction
edited by Glenwood Irons
(University of Toronto Press, 1995)
Murder by the Book? by Sally Munt
(Routledge, 1994)
Detective Agency
by Priscilla Walton and Manina Jones
(University of California Press)

Gill Plain

Gill Plain is a lecturer in English at the University of St Andrews. She works on twentieth-century popular fiction and film, and her recent publications include *Twentieth-century Crime Fiction: Gender, Sexuality and the Body* (Edinburgh University Press, 2001), and *Ian Rankin's Black and Blue* (Continuum, 2002).

SUE GRAFTON AND THE NEW WOMAN DETECTIVE

Susan Rowland

Sue Grafton's PI, Kinsey Millhone is usually linked with Marcia Muller's Sharon McCone and Sara Paretsky's V I Warshawski as the new American tough-gal hardboiled sleuths. Each of them narrates her own story making a 'her' story of the previously male dominated genre. Starting out in *A is for Alibi* in 1986, Kinsey stands out from the other two by fidelity to her personal style. While all three deploy the standard integrity that marks the loner detective out from the petty corruptions of modern urban life, Kinsey is still taking the unglamorous cases of her early days. Whereas all three professional women maintain deep friendships, are loyal to colleagues, build up alternative families and would never, ever, get sucked into organised crime, Kinsey alone remains the same sort of detective. Sharon McCone has gravitated from a legal co-operative to the kind of crimes where the detective actually *needs* her personal plane and even V I is dipping her toe into the perilous waters of transnational and even transhistorical evil (e.g. the Nazi atrocities in *Total Recall*). Kinsey's mean streets are those of the working and professional classes of Santa Theresa, fictional Californian smallish seaside town. Her latest adventure in *Q is for Quarry* sees her taking down market office space and helping out an ailing cop. The two strike up an alliance to re-open an ancient case involving an unidentified local corpse. And here's another thing about Kinsey – she likes cops. Santa Theresa's finest are hard working guys (no women?) who find it easy to respect Kinsey. Here she differs again from the more tortuous love-hate relationship that V I has with Chicago. Grafton gets away with her distinctively corrupt-free police by insisting that Santa Theresa is too small for major league betrayal. Her novels are of small town urban decay and crime. True, Kinsey occasionally gets drawn out to the desert, as in *G is for Gumshoe,* or into the big west coast cities in pursuit of a lost Theresan soul, such as in *H is for Homicide* when Kinsey is more or less kidnapped and taken to Los Angeles. And even in Santa Theresa, it has been known for a dark expensive car to draw up as the Mafia reveals that its reach is everywhere. However, mostly, Kinsey patrols the surprisingly dark alleys of the modern American family, the true 'home' of murder.

Kinsey's lack of desire to change her modus operandi matches her intensely independent private life. Lodger in a tiny apartment with an octogenarian landlord, Henry Pitts, Kinsey knows that her love for small cramped spaces is a legacy from her childhood. Both her parents were killed in a car crash in which she became trapped in the mangled vehicle. Raised by unsentimental Aunt Gin, Kinsey's early life was difficult. Two failed marriages are mentioned and although Kinsey has an on-off relationship with fellow private eye Robert Dietz, her usual mode of living is solitary. After a spell in the police force, Kinsey prefers to work alone. In this she is both like and unlike her male predecessors. Typically, the male hardboiled investigator is a loner with a dysfunctional sex life. His basic decency usually shows up the cops as institutionally corrupt. They are an aspect of the big bad city that one well-meaning intrinsically good guy has to endure rather than cure. Kinsey is different. Her inhibitions about relationships have defined limits. After all, she gets involved with the lives of her friends, usually to good effect, and her men tend to have well advertised drawbacks – like a wife who periodically leaves and returns in the case of cop, Jonah Robb, and Dietz's even more emphatic refusal to be tied down. Kinsey knows that she ends up with uncommitted men because the one thing she most avoids is the typical female role of housewife. She has a history to her horror of full-time domesticity and is a victim of trauma rather than of the contradictions of modern urban masculinity. Another untypical feature of Kinsey and Santa Theresa is the localisation of sin. Murders are the result of criminality at once more individual and general. On the one hand the typical killer is no crazed serial slayer à la Cornwell. He or she is usually a petty criminal entangled in an increasing web of deceit that often started with a venial or financial white collar crime. Often a family has decayed to the point of implosion as in the ghastly legatees in *M is for Malice*. On the other hand, Grafton presents a world in entropy. Although Kinsey succeeds in bonding with a few good hearted individuals in every story (and some of them come in unconventional packages like the appealing child-woman prostitute in *K is for Killer*), she discovers each time a society in decline, unsure of its values and easily seduced into taking risks with the law.

This pervasive American moral weakness is matched and in part communicated through settings. Pursuit of justice, or at least the unreliable guidance of her clients takes Kinsey onto seedy joints, cheap housing with seniors on declining incomes, the non-working poor, or for those convinced they can buy their way through social inconveniences, the empty architecture of men whose aging wives sip away afternoons from tall glasses by the pool. Kinsey drives (everywhere) amongst the landscape of cheap motels on the edge of deserts, gas stations, all-night coffee shops, depressed malls with trash scattered about, houses gently mouldering into the pacific; the battle with devouring nature already lost and fought without grace. If the poor seem to have diminished lives in Santa Theresa, then the rich appear to be even more quietly desperate. This is a world with constant good weather, no hunger and the freedom to shut the door on the wider community. No one reads or thinks about politics beyond the town boundary. Local elections are about favours needed to build yet another tasteless monstrosity as a machine for making money. It is a society that has escaped the constricting values of the past and has only divorce and ubiquitous TV to put in its place. The American dream has soured a little and few can be bothered to remember what it was all about. So unsurprisingly heroes are few and far between with those who try to uphold the law in an indifferent, almost apathetic town, picked out as the good guys.

Just as Kinsey drives around a decaying American twilight, so Grafton takes risks in depicting this criminal milieu of relentless ordinariness. Fortunately, the gallant detective discovers that crime peels away the fast food wrapping of her world to reveal something darker, chaotic, mixing veniality with violence and horror. A decayed body has "small white maggots [that] glowed like a spray of seed pearls". If the corpse is the ultimate sign of the abyss under the banal veneer of small town USA, then this perverse beauty is a trace of its seductive power. One of the best novels to see this is *K is for Killer*. Here Kinsey's investigation not only brings the standard dead body of the opening pages to imaginative life, it also threatens to turn the detective into some sort of avenging vampire. In a satisfyingly typical opening, Janice Kepler asks Kinsey to investigate the unsolved murder of her youngest daughter, another almost perversely independent young woman called Lorna. The one jarring note in the picture of an unremarkable respectable family is that Janice has been sent a porn film starring the victim. Soon Kinsey discovers that Lorna does not resemble the bland vacuity of her jealous sisters. A very expensive prostitute by night, part-time clerk by day, Lorna was a loyal friend who was tragically addicted to danger. Drawn into her darkening world, Kinsey herself starts to live and work at night, discovering her own personality undergo startling shifts. She befriends Hector, a night radio host whose magnificent beast of a dog howls like a soul in hell when she smells Lorna's scent on Kinsey. Normally a scrupulous respecter of others boundaries, Kinsey questions cop, Cheney Philips, about his expensive background. Together Philips and Kinsey are drawn to hooker, Danielle, the child-woman who gives Kinsey lessons on financial management and, at last, a decent hair cut. It is the hair cut that gives the tough-minded reader a clue about the fate of Danielle. Rarely does Kinsey let anyone get that close. *K is for Killer* begins with an evocation of the murdered whose killers go free: "[the] victims of unresolved homicides I think of as the unruly dead; restless, dissatisfied, longing for release." By the end of the novel Kinsey has taken one step into the land of the ghouls. Feeling she may be "turning into a vampire or a werewolf... seduced by the moon", she can only avoid the ultimate identification with two murder victims by becoming an indirect killer herself.

Another recent tale to challenge Kinsey's narrative of herself is *O is for Outlaw*, which brings her back into the orbit of her second husband, a cop known as Mickey. Characteristically, the start of the case finds Kinsey picking over someone's discarded household oddments, only these are her own, and appear to represent the remains of her ex-husband's life. Kinsey discovers an unopened letter addressed to her. She had left her marriage because she believed that Mickey was trying to use her to falsify an alibi for the beating of a suspect who subsequently died. The letter appears to clear him of the worst aspects of the crime and induces Kinsey to try to track him down. One of the old 'friends' Kinsey encounters is Dixie, author of the letter, lover of Mickey, who accuses Kinsey of a lack of loyalty and faith in Mickey. Certainly, throughout *O is for Outlaw*, Kinsey finds it easier to kindle a bond with Mickey as a crime victim and centre of a mystery than for someone with whom she shared domesticity. It is telling too, that the novel immediately prior to *O is for Outlaw* is one where Kinsey is most isolated and friendless. *N is for Noose* sees Kinsey drawn to the rural Nota Lake, a town so named for its legendary habit of branding criminals. Unfortunately, Kinsey's path to investigating the troubled last days of decent cop Tom Newquist is frustrated by the propensity of the unfriendly locals to 'brand' Kinsey as trouble. She even gets shot by her own client and the identification of a double murderer is left even more unsatisfying as usual. With insufficient evidence of homicide, the guilty party is likely to evade justice in the matter of trying to kill Kinsey. No one much cares and the town is (perversely) glad to see her go. Here, Kinsey suffers the true fate of the hardboiled private eye: to find out the truth (mostly) yet fail in the matter of healing society.

Kinsey's good endings come from an establishment of intimacy with the dead. A good example is the unexpected 'hero' and victim of *M is for Malice*, Guy Malek. Despite his hellraiser past, Guy fulfils an optimistic Grafton type, the teenager rebel who learns responsibility. Now a Christian, Guy's affection for Kinsey enables her to finally let go of her inner ghosts. In a novel that starts with Kinsey's uncanny double, a cousin Tasha from the extended family that has ignored her and who resembles her physically rather than emotionally (and she has an anti-Kinsey life as a smart lawyer), the tale ceases when Kinsey feels released from grieving over the wraiths of her dead parents and aunt. The fact that tender Guy rather than brisk Tasha achieves this for Kinsey suggests that the road to familial encounters will be rocky. I can't wait for the first meeting with imperious 'Grand', Millhone matriarch. *T is for Tyrant* anyone?

Susan Rowland

Susan Rowland's latest book is From Agatha Christie to Ruth Rendell *(Palgrave)*

SUE GRAFTON: A IS FOR ALPHABET

Mark Campbell

There cannot be many crime writers with the commitment – some might say the madness – to base a series of books around each and every letter of the alphabet. But that's just what Kentucky-born Sue Grafton has chosen to do, starting off with A is for Alibi *in 1982. Now on the home stretch (only nine more letters to go!), she took time out from her alphabet-obsessed writing career to talk to* Crime Time *about the concept for the series and the inspiration for the newest entry,* Q is for Quarry.

Q is for Quarry is based on a true story, isn't it?

Yes, it's based on a homicide that took place in Lompoc, California – an hour north of Santa Barbara – in August of 1969. I heard about the case because I was at a dinner party and sat down next to a man named Dr Robert Failing who'd been a coroner on the case at that time. And he remarked to me that it had always puzzled him that this girl was never identified, because her teeth were so odd. He said in passing (one of those sentences you later thank the heavens for), "You know,

we still have her maxilla and mandible. Would you like to see them?" Well...! He took me to the coroner's office and introduced me to some of the Santa Barbara County Sheriff's Department detectives and from that point on I began to create a story using as much of the original detail as I could.

Is it important to you that this mystery is wrapped up?

Well, in all my years of working on the series I had never done a story from an actual case. So although it was just a book project, I learnt so much police procedure and made such valuable contacts, and we became so caught up in the story of this young woman and the fact that she was still unidentified to this day, in the end it became a much more personal story for me.

It must have been a special book to write.

Yes it was – but she has still not been identified. I understand from the Santa Barbara County Sheriff's Department that they've had 25 or 30 leads since the book was published. I think people want to be helpful, but they often misunderstand these things. For instance, I got a couple of letters from people who had seen a woman who'd gone missing as recently as 1985, even though there's no doubt whatsoever that the woman I wrote about was found dead in August 1969!

Was it always mooted for the alphabet series or did you think about writing a stand-alone novel?

No, I'm really committed to doing the alphabet – but I may be committed to a mental asylum as soon as I've finished it! I am always looking for some new way to tell a story, because when you make a commitment to do 26 novels you'd better find a way to make each one interesting and done right. So from my perspective it's just a wonderful opportunity to do something different.

Did you just like the sound of *A is for Alibi*, or was it a conscious decision to sit down and write 26 books?

Well, my father had published a couple of mysteries, two books of a rejected eight-book series based on a British nursery rhyme about an old lady trying to get a pig over a stile. His two books were *The Rat Began to Gnaw the Rope* and *The Rope Began to Hang the Butcher*. That's when I thought, "Hey, what a keen idea". He was bright enough to figure out that a publisher would like to have some way of cueing the public into the fact that a writer had a new book out. I'd been hoping to find a way to link titles, and obviously I knew about John D McDonald, and Harry Kemelman, who linked his books with days of the week. I was reading an Edward Gorey cartoon book called *The Gashly Crumb Tinies* – they're a little series of rhymes that look like pen and ink drawings of Victorian children being done in in various ways: 'A is for Amy who fell down the stairs', 'B is for Basil who was assaulted by bears'. And I thought, "Hot damn! Have I got it!"

The alphabet concept is a great idea, because it's a commitment for you and for the publisher and the readers.

Everyone's in it for the long haul.

Exactly. It's also helpful to me to have an infrastructure. By using the actual case-files it gave me a very specific starting point, and then my job was to sit down and imagine what this woman's life had been like and how she might have ended up as a private eye in California.

So this is the only book you've based on true events?

I will occasionally use a snippet from a piece of paper, but I'm always worried about being sued! So I tend to restrict myself to the stories that are wholly invented. Although reality being such, just about anything you make up has actually happened in the world.

In 1983 you wrote teleplays for two Christie stories, *A Caribbean Mystery* and *Sparkling Cyanide* – was that fun?

Yes. Oddly enough though, Agatha Christie is very difficult to convert to the screen. I don't know why, but often if you were to take those stories apart and dissect them in the way you would have to do for a screenplay, there would be certain elements that didn't quite hold together, so it was always a challenge to make her come to life on the screen. Now also, as I understand it, her estate did not sell the best of her books to television – they would sell those off to film companies.

Let's turn to your working habits. I've heard you talk about something called your Shadow – could you elaborate?

Yes. I learnt about the difference between Shadow and Ego when I was working on *J is for Judgement*. The writing had become flat. I had become a good girl scout, I would set my marks, I was doing everything I was supposed to do, but I was just unhappy and it was showing up in the work. So somebody recommended a therapist who did Yin Yang therapy. I met the man once and after that I dealt with him once a week on the phone, because he was down in Los Angeles and I was in Santa Barbara, and in three months he taught me so much. Everything I use today is from this man. But it was odd to me because I had been accustomed to what I call 'boo hoo therapy', where you'd bemoan your early childhood and weep and all this stuff – it's so pointless! – and when he taught me it always seemed very academic and intellectual. I couldn't believe it was going to be helpful, but actually it just turned my work around. For one thing, it's Ego that worries about failing, Shadow doesn't care about that, she just wants to tell a story and have a good time. So I gave up any hopes of succeeding and just decided to write with the freedom I started with.

So your initial freedom had faded away and left you working with energy that wasn't there.

That's exactly it. After a while I learnt to trust myself and my instincts, and the notion that somebody else might not like it and might not approve, well, it's like, "Who cares?"

Almost like guided writing, as if your pen is the channel for the story?

Exactly. And what I discovered, and it's been true for many years since then, is that there's a little piece of you that always knows what the story is; so my job as a writer is to just keep tapping into that without regard for anything except the work itself.

But surely you're at such a stage now where readers' opinions don't matter as much as they used to?

Oh, they certainly do. For one thing, I never quite think of myself as successful. I'm always working on the book that's going to kill me, the book that's going to be the end of my career. And this adds a certain amount of tension. For another, just yesterday I answered five or six letters from readers, most of whom were writing in with minor corrections. Some people get infuriated by typos, it's like the end of the world for them. They send me these elaborate letters with page and line notes about grammatical errors and typos, and some of them were very helpful because we were just about to go into the printing process for the paperback and I just got a few corrections in, just in the nick of time. Some of them we'd already caught, but some we hadn't noticed. So readers are alert, they are detail-orientated and they are opinionated. I find that helpful.

Have you ever had any direct inspiration from a reader for one of your books?

I had an inspiration from a private investigator I worked with, who happened to be a reader of mine, and that was for *I is for Innocent*. I met this man when I was researching *C is for Corpse*, and he talked in passing (it's always those passing remarks!) about this civil murder trial where an accused has been acquitted of a crime, but then relatives of the victim had gone back into the civil court and sued for wrongful death. That was the framework I used for *I is for Innocent*. It was essentially what happened with OJ Simpson.

Do you ever have trouble remembering the titles of your books?

Oh yeah. People write and say, "What was this about?" and I have to write back and say, "You're asking the wrong person!"

Ask another reader!

Exactly. There is a book called *G is for Grafton,* which was written by two scholars from the University of South Carolina, and I use that as a resource! Often they have chronological sequences of events that are very helpful to me.

You've been quoted as saying that Kinsey Millhone is essentially a younger you, or a younger you if you'd chosen a different career path.

I describe her as the person I might have been had I not married young and had children.

Realistically, do you think you might have become a private detective?

That I don't know about. I grew up in the 1950s and 60s, and women, as I look back on it, never seemed to do anything very interesting back then. I never even *knew* women could be private investigators. Now many women have moved into the field. You'll find many who work as police officers, they're judges, they're attorneys, and they're certainly private investigators. So I think were I growing up in this day and age it would certainly be something that would interest me. Whether you could make a living at it, I don't know. But I happened to make the right choice for me.

So you're very happy with what you're doing?

I am. Well, very happy in that I'm on the brink of disaster at all times!

What will you do to celebrate when you get to Z?

When I get to *Z is for Zero*? I'm not sure. It won't happen till the year 2015 and I keep telling people, "Do you know what you're going to do in 2015?"

You can plan ahead!

Yeah. I will have other tales to tell though. It's possible Kinsey Millhone and I will have other business together. But I will never, ever link titles again – I don't know what I was thinking! [*Laughs*] I will go to any lengths to do stand-alone books, because you can have the freedom to do it once and then back off.

The future is obviously healthy for you – do you think it's healthy for crime fiction in general?

Yes, I do. I am not pretending to be a prognosticator, I don't know what the future holds any more than anybody else does, but certainly I think there is a growing awareness of crime and law enforcement and the process by which people are brought to justice, and I think there is an awakening in the public, at least in this country, to taking some responsibility for seeing that culprits are brought to justice. In America we have a lot of police procedural shows, crime scene investigation shows, that sort of thing, and that can only help the mystery writer, whose bread and butter is based on the same information.

And of course it's important to see justice done in the books, isn't it?

Yes, because it doesn't happen that often in real life.

Lastly, your current hardback shows you sitting in an armchair in the middle of the road. Is this a normal part of your working day?

[*Laughs*] That road was so heavily populated, every time a number of trucks passed we had to haul the chair off the road and let them go by. We had two highway patrol officers walking traffic – how I managed to look relaxed I do not know. But I'll tell you the good news about it. A woman who worked for Saucony, who make the running shoes, noticed that I was wearing Saucony trainers in that photograph and sent me a free pair!

Mark Campbell

Sue Grafton is published by Macmillan

SUE GRAFTON BIBLIOGRAPHY

compiled by Mark Campbell

Sue Taylor Grafton was born on 24 April 1940 in Louisville, Kentucky, the daughter of attorney/mystery writer C W Grafton. She received a BA in English from the University of Louisville in 1961 and 17 years later married Steven Frederick Humphrey. Together they co-wrote many successful scripts for American television. Grafton achieved worldwide success in 1982 with the first of her alphabetical mystery stories featuring wisecracking private eye Kinsey Millhone. To date the 17 novels have been translated into the following languages: Bulgarian, Chinese, Croatian, Czech, Danish, Dutch, Finnish, French, German, Hebrew, Icelandic, Indonesian, Italian, Japanese, Korean, Norwegian, Polish, Portuguese, Spanish and Swedish. She is the recipient of two Shamus Awards, four Anthony Awards, two American Mystery Awards and seven Doubleday Mystery Guild Awards. She has been President of the Private Eye Writers of America (1989/90) and the Mystery Writers of America Inc. (1994/95). As if that's not enough, she has given lectures on writing in California, Ohio, New Mexico, Washington DC and Wyoming. She has three children, Leslie, Jay and Jamie, from previous marriages, as well as two granddaughters, Erin and the appropriately named Kinsey. She shares her time between homes in Louisville and Montecito, California, and cites cats, gardens and good cuisine as favourite pastimes.

Novels

The Alphabet Series

Q is for Quarry (2002)
P is for Peril (2001)
O is for Outlaw (1999)
N is for Noose (1998)
[Friends of the Library USA Award]
M is for Malice (1996)
[Doubleday Mystery Guild Award]
L is for Lawless (1995)
K is for Killer (1994) [Shamus Award]
J is for Judgement (1993)
[Doubleday Mystery Guild Award]
I is for Innocent (1992) [Doubleday Mystery Guild & American Mystery Awards]
H is for Homicide (1991) [Doubleday Mystery Guild & American Mystery Awards]
G is for Gumshoe (1990) [Doubleday Mystery Guild, Anthony & Shamus Awards]
F is for Fugitive (1989) [Doubleday Mystery Guild & Falcon Awards]
E is for Evidence (1988)
[Doubleday Mystery Guild Award]
D is for Deadbeat (1987)
C is for Corpse (1986) [Anthony Award]
B is for Burglar (1985)

[Shamus & Anthony Awards]
A is for Alibi (1982)
[Mysterious Stranger Award]

Others

The Lolly-Madonna War (1969)
Keziah Dane (1967)

Kinsey Millhone Short Stories

Kinsey and Me: Collected Short Stories (1992)
Non Sung Smoke (1988)
The Parker Shotgun (1986)
[Macavity & Anthony Awards]
Murder Between the Sheets (1986)
She Didn't Come Home (1986)

Other Short Stories

A Little Missionary Work (1992)
Full Circle (1991)
A Poison that Leaves no Trace (1990)
[American Mystery Award]
Falling Off the Roof (1989)

Film

Lolly-Madonna XXX (with Rodney Carr-Smith, from the author's own book, 1973)

Television

Tonight's the Night
(with Steven Humphrey, 1987)
The Canterville Ghost
(with Steven Humphrey, from the play by Oscar Wilde, 1986)
Love on the Run
(with Steven Humphrey, 1985)
Sparkling Cyanide (with Steven Humphrey, from the book by Agatha Christie, 1983)
A Caribbean Mystery (with Steven Humphrey & Robert Malcolm Young, from the book by Agatha Christie, 1983)
A Killer in the Family
(with Steven Humphrey, 1983)
Seven Brides for Seven Brothers
(with Steven Humphrey, pilot and two episodes from series, 1982/83)
Mark, I Love You
(from the book by Hal Painter, 1980)
Nurse
(from the book by Peggy Anderson, 1980)
Sex and the Single Parent
(from the book by Jane Adams, 1979)
Walking Through the Fire (from the book by Laurel Lee, 1979) [Christopher Award]
Rhoda (episode 'With Friends Like These', 1975)

Honours

Guest of Honour, Bouchercon, Washington DC (2001)
Induction American Academy of Achievement, Phoenix Arizona (2000)
Guest of Honour, Murder in the Grove, Boise, Idaho (2000)
Guest of Honour, Left Coast Crime, Tucson, Arizona (2000)
Honouree, GALA Fourteen, Birmingham-Southern College (1999)
Mystery Masters Award, Magna Cum Murder, Ball State University (1998)
Honorary Doctorate of Literature, Western Maryland College (1998)
Alumna of the Year, University of Louisville (1997)
Distinguished Alumna, University of Louisville (1993)

Reference

G is for Grafton: The World of Kinsey Millhone by Natalie Hevener Kaufman & Carol McGinnis Kay (Henry Holt, 1997, £11.99) gives you the rundown of every last plot twist and character nuance from her first 15 novels. For online information, visit Sue Grafton's own website at www.suegrafton.com

Mark Campbell

WHY WAS TERRY QUINN KILLED?

George P Pelecanos *talks to Matt Levy*

How did you get into writing books? How did you start?

The first thing I ever tried to write was my first novel. I just had a book in my head for a long time – ten years! I just decided to give it a try; just one book was my ambition. But I had no knowledge of how to do it, or the business. I hadn't even met an author before. I wrote it all in longhand – twice – and then bought a computer and did a third draft over a year. I then sent it to one publisher and because I'd read in the *Writers' Handbook* that I could only send the manuscript to one publisher at a time that's what I did. Of course, it's done so there's no bidding war, but I thought it was decorum so that was fine. I didn't follow it up – I forgot about it. I enjoyed the experience so much I just wrote another. One year later I heard back. They picked it off the slush pile and a junior editor liked it and made me an offer. I was into my second book at the time and since then, I've written one every year.

So you like doing one a year?

Yes. But I'm not a brand name yet! My publishers are happy though, put it that way.

Therefore, there was no specific character or event that inspired you?

That's right. I wanted to make movies and got a degree in it, but like many people I thought afterwards, 'now what?'. But while at university I was turned onto books by a professor. Beforehand I wasn't into reading. I became interested in hard-boiled detective fiction – Chandler, McDonald and others – and it was like a light bulb went on over my head. These books were about my world – the literature of the working class. I got into these kind of books and slowly I thought, well, I'm from this world, I can do it. But it took ten years of making up for lost time.

You're known as a writer who transcends genres. Having read *Shame the Devil* there's a mass appeal; but characterisation is vital in all novels. Tell me about Derek Strange, Nick Stefanos and Terry Quinn.

Nick Stefanos was me, you know? Drinking, getting high every day. I found writing and a family that meant a lot more to me. I'm not against it but at that point I had done it for so long the novelty had gone. Nick Stefanos didn't, and that's where our characters separate. He's a falling-down drunk in Down by the River Where the Dead Men Go. But he's always there. There are elements of Strange and Quinn in my character but they are the least autobiographical of anything I've ever done. They're composites of people I've known in DC. Especially Strange as a black man of a certain age and cultural experience that I've known. What's gratifying is that I'm not writing about myself anymore and the books are stronger. Strange is the best thing I've written and he's not me. You just want to get better. I'd be disappointed if my books now aren't as good as my early ones.

Why was Terry Quinn killed?

It's not something you'd do in a series – you're killing the goose that laid the golden egg and I can't bring him back. But it served the book [*Soul Circus*] and it made sense in the context of the book. It dovetailed into the themes of the story. If you're writing serious books, you know that it's bullshit in a way. If the reader is so comfortable with a character, and they know they're coming back in the next book, it's reality to the degree where it's no longer valid. Because we all live under the spectre of mortality. But though I didn't intend to kill him, it became clear about halfway through he was going to die. I knew my US publisher wouldn't like it but we had a meeting and they agreed to it. It couldn't end any other way. Stefanos will be back for sure, though!

Now that Terry's dead, you can develop Janine and Lionel...

Potentially, though my new book is set in 1968 when Derek was a policeman. I've been laying the foundation for it in all my books. I wanted to write a book set during the 1968 riots. There are hints in the books to this end.

Gangs are dealt with in *Soul Circus*. Do you consider yourself to be an educator?

I consider my work to be almost journalistic – fictional reportage. A lot of people even in DC don't know the type of characters in *Soul Circus*. They lock their doors when they drive through the neighbourhood and if a kid's killed he gets a buried paragraph in the newspaper. It's like they're not human.

You point out that some of the people in their life are criminals. But are they forced into it?

Yes. It's an accident of birth; they were born in a place they didn't choose. It's all environment. If you think they're animals, you're dead wrong. If they were born on the other side of town they'd be doctors or lawyers or whatever. And because it's environmental we can do something about it if we choose. Don't write them off – they are human and I try and give them dimension in my book. If you finish my book and think, 'there's something going on that I've been ignoring', that's great. I don't have the answers – I'm just trying to raise a bunch of questions.

Derek Strange coaches a football team to help the kids. Is that how you draw attention to the social situation in DC?

The team in the books is like a team my sons play on – most of the kids don't have one or both of their parents around and are going the wrong way. Something can be done, but because the government won't do anything, it has to come from the community. There are people valiantly trying to keep it together and these people are heroes, man. It's not just sports coaches but people who work in churches and community groups and stuff like that who put something back.

What's your view on access to firearms in the US?

We have a strong tradition of gun culture in this country going back to the constitution. You couple that with a US trait of mistrust of the law and that's why people want to own guns in case the guys in boots come knocking on your door. You see, there are people who want to ban all guns but realistically it'll never happen. And then there are people like the NRA who have the politicians in their pocket. I'm not optimistic about rational gun control happening here because the system is corrupt.

Terry's killed because he went back to his witness with a gun, which leads to him being chased down and shot. There's a lesson there to walk away...

Exactly. You can't perpetuate this madness with the guns, you know? Terry has always had an issue with his masculinity and pride and he goes back too many times. Like in *Hell to Pay* when he goes back to the pimp, Worldwide Wilson. He pushes it one too many times in Soul Circus. How many times can these guys go into battle and come out unscarred? The majority of police don't pull their weapons in their whole career. But there's another lesson too; there are all these books with private detectives shooting people left and right. It's not realistic!

Speaking of realism, when you were looking to create Derek, it's almost as if you were a PI yourself...

These books are almost how it really is for a private investigator. I wanted this trilogy to be the way it is. When Strange opens his trunk and I describe his tools, that's what a PI carries. I rode with these guys for quite a bit and worked in their offices. I made notes on the things they carried; but I was committed to one thing – that Derek would never pick up or use a gun. As a genre writer you're putting up a big wall because he doesn't go in guns blazing. So how do you make it exciting? You make the conflict as part of the plot.

In *Soul Circus* he uses a knife, though. That was unusual...

He kind of loses it – he's human, remember. It was almost childish. He cuts Horace McKinley's nipple off! Everyone has their breaking point – even Derek. He becomes militant at the end of the book when the death of Terry, his friend pushes Derek over the edge and he burns the gun shop down.

Speaking of which, *Hell to Pay* was very emotional, wasn't it, with the child getting killed...

Yes. The murder is based on and dedicated to the case of a seven-year-old kid who was shot dead here in DC. But when Derek finds the killers, he spares them. Most people want to see those guys killed in the worst possible way. Are you dissatisfying readers by sparing the murderers? But it's what Strange would have done. Their lives are fucked anyhow – it was written in stone long before they were caught and they'd have died in prison.

***Shame the Devil* was very intense. Does writing like that take it out of you?**

For sure. It's not fun writing about the death of a kid, that's for sure. But the impetus for that book was these sexual murders in Washington called the Starbucks Murders. These guys broke into a Starbucks before it opened, took everyone in the back and killed them. There was a lot of media and the Washington Press did an article on one of the girls who was killed who was coming out; she was gay. I was thinking, would she want these details in the papers? What I'm saying is that most books have things put back in order at the end. But in reality, that's not true. If someone's killed violently then the family and friends have to live with it for the rest of their lives. You can't solve a murder unless you bring the victim back. *Shame the Devil* is about finding spirituality in a violent world – themes you wouldn't discuss in a crime novel.

Frank Farrow was a psycho, though... I was pleased he was killed!

Yeah, he was irredeemable. He's one of the few guys I've ever written about who's bad all the way through and someone like that has to die.

Now: about yourself. Tell me about your day.

It's very regimented. First I go out and do my research which can be a month or two months of street research, interviews and library work. I don't break to write, then go out and research. When I do start to write, I write every day, seven days a week until the book's done. I'll work in the morning, have a late lunch and rewrite in the evening what I did earlier so the very next morning I'm ready to go forward. It only takes five months to write a book, but it's very intense.

Do you use the same information sources for your books?

Yes, there's quite a few I use or I call them to get me new people. For example, with *Soul Circus* I was with the Alcohol, Tobacco and Firearms Unit because they know everything about the gun trade and how it works. It's got easier because I'm a bit more well known and people will take my calls.

What about prison visits? You mentioned street contacts...

I've done that. Information gets offered to me. People call me and say, "I've read your book. I was in the drug game for ten years. If you need any help...". They want to get on the straight and narrow and that's the best type of call I can get. One thing I will say is that I only write about what I know. I'd never write about being in prison, for example. If you don't know what you're talking about, the readers know pretty quickly. I don't have the imagination to write about what I don't know; everything in my books comes from what I've experienced. I couldn't create a female protagonist, for example, because I don't know what it's like to be a woman!

Are you worried about the future of DC?

You've got to be optimistic or you can't get up in the morning. There'll always be an underclass. When you live in a capitalist society you'll have people who are left behind. It's your responsibility as a citizen to look after them. They talk about war in Iraq and defending Americans but it doesn't apply to all Americans apparently. There are kids in Mr Bush's own city who are going to bed hungry.

Some of the quotes you get from other authors like Michael Connelly are terrific. How does it feel to be friends and rivals?

Well, Mike and I tour together – he's a great guy. When he does well I'm happy. He's another level up from me. I don't think, if Mike sold 100,000 fewer copies, maybe I'll get some of them. He's up with authors like Stephen King. As for quotes, I got one from Elmore Leonard and was honoured.

How do you relax? Do you switch off?

Well, I don't have any hobbies. I love watching sports on TV especially football and basketball. I love films, of course. But at the moment I'm so busy – *The Wire*, a one-hour drama I've written is coming to the UK soon. We're shooting the second series so I go to work every day. I don't need it but I've got a full-time job. I'm also doing author tours, and then I finish the TV show before starting another book! Maybe one day I'll take a breath and have a break but I'm having a great time. I work from home so I see my family as much as I want. It's a good life and I wouldn't trade it for anything.

Matt Levy

George Pelecanos is published by Orion

INTERVIEW

THE IRREVERSIBLE MR TUROW

***Barry Forshaw** meets Scott Turow*

It's not that easy to virtually hijack a genre, but the crown prince of the sharply written legal thriller is no longer John Grisham (since his born-again Christianity has crept into his work and vitiated it); it's the mordantly talented Scott Turow. Best known for *Presumed Innocent* (and its concomitant movie), along with four other highly successful novels, Turow has again produced in *Reversible Errors* the kind of work his admirers turn to him for: machine-tooled plotting, gritty and plausible legal detail (we expect no less from the author) and a cold-eyed, dispassionate examination of human behaviour. If this new one breaks no boundaries, it displays Turow's skills at their most refined and impressive. Rommy 'Squirrel' Gandolph is due to be executed for a multiple murder he had been convicted of ten years previously. As the time of the lethal appointment ticks ever closer, corporate lawyer Arthur Raven finds himself appointed by the court to represent Gandolph after a surprise not-guilty plea. Raven finds that there is new evidence, but the whole implacable legal machine (and public opinion) has hardened against any revisionism: Rommy Gandolph will die, and no legal niceties will postpone that. But another prisoner, terminally ill with cancer, has some important information, and Raven finds unlikely aid from a retired judge and a recovering drug addict. Kindle County, the milieu here, is conjured with a precision that's every inch the equal of Turow's adroit characterisation. Tackling once again the collision of ordinary human existence and the exigencies of the legal apparatus, Turow vividly brings to life not just the beleaguered attorney who is his protagonist, but also the hate-filled characters who populate this heady narrative. You may be tired of legal thrillers – but here's one to remind you why this genre got so damned popular.

Scott Turow is in London to promote

his new novel *Reversible Errors* (Picador), and for the jaded *Crime Time* journo (who has perhaps spoken to too many none-too-bright American authors), it's a refreshing change to encounter a writer whose personable qualities are matched by a sharp intelligence. The conversation ranges over many issues (with his best-selling novels being only one among many topics), and it's hard to know what to spotlight first. How, for instance, does Turow regard his putative readers? "I take my readers as I find them", says Turow. "There are those who are looking for a page-turning thriller: fine. Some want plausible details of how the courts and the lawyers work: I'm pleased to have them on board too." So why do we continue to have a fascination for the legal profession while regarding lawyers as something akin to pond life? "I think there is a plurality of values here", replies the author. "The law is the arbiter of values. And of course we're all cynical when there is a clear miscarriage of justice, for instance, when the OJ trial came to its famously controversial conclusion, many people were outraged. But, on the other hand, if you're being prosecuted for a major crime, who are you going to call? Johnnie Cochran, of course!" Is Turow worried by the fact that so many legal thrillers are clogging up bookshops? "I don't think the market is in danger of being swamped yet. There appears to be a stable level of high interest, and, for the time being readers still seem fascinated by the genre." Turow enthusiastically talks about his faith in science, and is dismissive of the idea that America is rushing headlong toward a kind of dumbed-down religious state. "I think the religious right is in the minority, and they get more column inches than they actually deserve. Fortunately, most of us are more concerned with science. I have a great faith in DNA, fingerprinting, ballistics – the latter is a key element in *Reversible Errors* if you'll forgive the plug." Inevitably, we touch on the Hollywood success of *Presumed Innocent*. "All my books have been optioned", says Turow, "and that's both a good and bad thing. After seeing the film of *Presumed Innocent*, I have to confess that Harrison Ford's face became mentally overlaid for me over that of my protagonist. But in the end, it's the book that counts, isn't it?"

Barry Forshaw

Reversible Errors is published by Picador

HARD FEELINGS

Jason Starr

My latest book in the UK is the mass market paperback edition of *Hard Feelings*. It's about a computer networking salesman whose marriage is going downhill and he becomes obsessed with a repressed memory – so it's another one of my lighthearted comedies. No Exit is bringing out all of my books in affordable, cool-looking mass market editions, and I'm really excited about that. I've been wanting my books to get into mass market for a long time.

I was influenced by the noir writers from the 1940s, 50s and 60s of course – Thompson, Cain, Goodis, Willeford, etc. But when I first started writing, in college, I hadn't read much crime fiction so I don't think I was as influenced 'as a writer' by these guys I mentioned. When I started writing my favourite writers were Hemingway, Carver, Cheever, and Salinger.

I have a couple of early novels in the drawer, as well as a couple of half-written and very poorly written – I can't even call them books – so let's just call them 'accumulations of sentences' which will remain unpublished forever. I do find that I go back to these books and pages unconsciously and pull out bits and pieces of them for other books, so I guess those efforts didn't go completely to waste. Now they're just source material.

I have some novel writing friends, and screenwriting friends, but I really work in isolation. I live in a neighbourhood in Manhattan where people are doctors, lawyers, or work in finance. I don't discuss my writing with anyone, even my wife, until I finish a book, so I just have a lot of stuff going on in my head. I hate discussing works in progress and I have a superstition that if I talk about an uncompleted work it will jinx it so I try to remain tightlipped.

My books have a lot of violence in them and why shouldn't they? What should I do, write about non-violent crime? There's nothing worse than a watered down crime novel. That said, I don't think I have gratuitous violence in my books. I think I describe violence in a very matter-of-fact, straightforward way – if you check out my new one, *Hard Feelings*, you'll see exactly what I mean. I try to right violence the way my characters experience it rather than to create cheap thrills. But to answer the question – no, I don't think writers, especially crime writers, should avoid violence, and they certainly shouldn't have violent scenes take place off stage.

I don't think there is any set rules for

how to write about sex. Part of the fun of writing is to try to come up with new ways of doing things. So if a writer can think of a great way to describe a sex scene, I say go for it. But if the sex scene is gratuitous, and doesn't seem to fit in with the overall writing in a book, I have a problem with that. For me, it depends on the book and the character I'm writing about. Bill Moss in *Cold Caller,* and David Sussman in *Nothing Personal* have perverted sides to themselves so I wrote sex scenes from their points of views. But I'm not gonna just stick sex scenes into my books for the hell of it.

Most of my characters don't usually care one way or the other about politics. They're way too self-absorbed.

I try to write for four hours a day every morning, but I have no set rules. Some days I don't write at all, some days I'll write in the morning and at night. I have a daughter I help raise so it's really a matter of whenever I can find free time. I usually write in a Starbucks or in a lounge in my building where I can plug in. The lounge has a great view of northern Manhattan so some days I just zone out, staring at the view, and don't write anything.

I hope that the appeal of my novels is to entertain. I have a fun time writing my books so I hope people get the same enjoyment out of reading them. At the same time, I hope my books aren't 'throw aways' that you can easily forget about. I hope people feel a little disturbed and icky after reading my books.

The average person is much more likely to see a movie than read a novel – at least that's the case with me. The mind naturally gravitates toward the easiest thing to do. So nowadays this means listen to music, go-online, watch TV, see a movie, read a book – in this order. So naturally writers, me included, see a lot of movies and this has to have an influence on writing. For me, music isn't as much of an influence, although when I have a character in a book who's into music, I'll have appropriate music references.

When I plot a story I usually think of a situation first, rather than a plot or character. For example, in *Hard Feelings*, I came up with the situation of a guy coming home from work and accidentally bumping into a guy whom he remembers later abused him when they were kids. I loved that idea and then fitting the character – Richard Segal, this pissed-off salesmen – into the plot made perfect sense.

Most of my books take place in New York because I like to write about what I know. I hate reading books that seem overly researched. Sure I'll do research when I don't know something, but I'm usu-

ally better off writing about what I know, or just making it up.

No Exit was my first publisher – they gave me my start as a writer, publishing me before I was published by anyone else, and they're the only publisher that has all of my books in print. It's hard to find dedication like that. I'm also fortunate to have great foreign publishers and to be published by Vintage Crime/Black Lizard in the US. I'm fortunate not to have had any bad experiences with any of my publishers yet. It's a far cry from my experiences in the movie business which has been full of drama and trouble.

I really don't think about the reader at all when I'm writing. I usually have so much on my mind I don't see how that could be possible.

Of course, reading is important these days. It's still the best form of entertainment because books are light, you can take them anywhere with you – even into the bathroom. If the book was invented today people would probably be going on about what a great breakthrough they are and there would probably be 'book stocks' selling for ridiculous prices on every stock exchange in the world. It's only because books have been around for so long that they get a bad rap.

These days writers are often promoted and packaged ahead of the actual books, but that's the way it is in all forms of entertainment. I recently wrote a screenplay for Halle Berry and the movie wouldn't have a chance of getting made if she didn't want to be in it. But it is annoying when you see a book in the store, written by some celebrity, and a publisher is giving it a lot of promotion only because of the star's name. People have so little time to read these days that when they do they should at least be reading good, well written books. I think publishers should have a moral responsibility to do this.

My next book in the UK will be *Tough Luck*. It's set in 1984, in Brooklyn, New York, and it's about a naïve guy who puts in some bets with his bookie, as a favour for a mob figure. The bets lose and the guy winds up in big debt to the mob guy's bookie. You might feel like crap for a while after you finish it, but hopefully you'll enjoy the ride.

All *Crime Time* readers are welcome at my home page: www.jasonstarr.com

Jason Starr

Hard Feelings *is published by No Exit Press*

NOIR FICTION: THE ANGUISH OF THE CURSED

***Paul Duncan** on writing Noir Fiction*

"A man who has become conscious of the absurd is forever bound to it. A man devoid of hope and is conscious of being so has ceased to belong to the future."

Notebooks by Albert Camus

"She felt a comfortable solidarity with the big company of the voluntary dead."

Big Blonde by Dorothy Parker

"There is nothing escapist about the black novel whatever. The writer cannot even escape himself in it; the black novel is the novel in which escape is shut off."

Derek Raymond

"All great literature is depressing."

Charles Willeford

I am not well. By that I mean that I am sick. Emotionally, physically, psychologically. The world is horrible. I wake in the morning, in my room, a small box at the end of a cement garden, and I look out at the black walls and grey skies, and I think myself better off in my room. Why do I need to go out there? What can I find out there that will make my life better? People? People are obnoxious, smelly, violent, impolite slabs of meat that travel from one place to another like ants following the invisible trails of their dead ancestors. They can teach me nothing – they do not know the things I know. No. I shall stay in my room and I will become pure. I will expel the filth that is within me, vomit up all the bad thoughts, the lifetime of programming that society imprints on my brain, and cleanse myself. I am not alone in my ideas. Many other writers think like me. Even in my putrid little room, I can hear the doubt in your minds. You want proof, you shall have proof. I will write it all down for you, so that you can see the world as it really is...

Noir is all those things we fear in the back of our minds, the parts of ourselves we want to block out because they make us feel uneasy. Noir doesn't always have pat solutions and attractive people, doesn't spoon-feed safe fantasies into drooling mouths. Noir drags you screaming and kicking through all sorts of hell before reaching some sort of unsatisfactory ending. It's not something that many people can take. Noir requires emotional commitment from the reader. The reader must be prepared to expose themselves to thoughts and feelings they'd rather not think or feel, and that's a hard thing to ask. At best, you can learn something about people and yourself. It all depends upon how much of the Noir you are willing to recognise in yourself. Noir is often associated with the crime, detective and thriller genres because they give ample opportunity for you to gaze into the minds of bad, dark people on the edge of society. There is little chance of these characters invading your secure privacy. This is the fallacy. These people are actually you. They live and express your secret desires, weaknesses, and motives. It is safer for the character to live for you than for you to admit your dark side to yourself. The crime, mystery, thriller and detective clichés are a code to protect you, a wall you build to stop yourself from being hurt. That's what *you* think...

Reading Noir is not a good experience. By that, I mean that when pouring over the black and white text of a Hardboiled or Action or Romance or Crime or Horror novel, there is a certain vicarious experience which leads to pleasure. You feel uplifted and alive. You wish to share the experience, the frisson, with your neighbour. After finishing a Noir novel, one is more likely to look upon their neighbour – if not with suspicion, then certainly with caution. Despite its name, Noir Fiction – or the Black Novel as some call it – is more likely to muddy the moral waters of our life rather than to make us see things clearly in black and white. Since it came into the English language in the mid-1980s, the word Noir has been used and abused. During the 1990s it became a buzzword, a designer label of a peculiar type of fiction that has black comedy apparel but rarely a heart of darkness. This has resulted in Tart Noir, Tartan Noir, Seaside Noir, Surf Noir and Country Noir among others. No doubt a book proclaiming itself part of the new Black Noir movement will soon find itself on the shelves. I can wait.

Let me make it clear, from the outset,

what this book is about. Noir is not a kind of macho Hardboiled fiction where Tough Guys pass moral judgement on an immoral society. Noir is about the weak-minded, the losers, the bottom-feeders, the obsessives, the compulsives and the psychopaths. Noir is not about the people standing on the edge of the abyss looking in, but about the people in it, forever writhing, aware of the pain, aware of the future pain to come. The character(s) must suffer/confront the darkness inside them. Whether they live or die is immaterial – the quest into this heart of darkness is the thing.

Definition

The word Hardboiled first appeared in cooking recipes of the 1730s to refer to hardboiled eggs. Mark Twain used it in 1886 to refer to rigid grammatical rules and by 1903, it was used to mean hard or stiff clothing such as the hat of a cowboy or the suits of travelling salesmen. By the end of World War One, it was commonly used to describe a rigid person, one who would not take a chance or relax a rule. It soon came to mean a person who was cynical, stoic and emotionally untouchable – the antithesis of Noir characters who are in constant pain and will tell the reader about it at the drop of a hat (hardboiled or not).

In America, the emotionally untouchable man was born in the popular myth of the American cowboy. He is a wanderer, a free spirit. It's hokum of course, but the myth evolved – the trail turned into the railroad, and later into the highway. The metaphor of travel was used as a device to describe and discover America. In the hands of Jack London and Jim Tully, the cowboy turned into the adventurer and the hobo. During the Depression, socialist writers like John Steinbeck led us down dust-bowl roads telling us about the bitter grapes of wrath, telling it like it was. Writers travelled the highways and byways, going walkabout to discover the world and themselves, to put themselves in touch with the masses, with society. In Britain, writers like George Orwell turned hobo to find out about the world they lived in. Some authors then began to use Private Investigators to comment on society. The earliest known PI story is *The Black Sleuth* by John E Bruce, which was serialised in *McGirt's Reader* from 1907 to 1909. However, the foremost exponent of the Hardboiled story was the *Black Mask* pulp magazine. The December 1922 issue fea-

tured the first Hardboiled stories: *The False Burton Combs* by Carroll John Daly and *The Road Home* by Peter Collinson (aka Dashiell Hammett). Dashiell Hammett and other American pulp writers of the 1920s wrote down what they heard on the streets. They used the voices of ordinary people for the first time. Also, from 1926, when Captain Joseph T Shaw became editor of *Black Mask*, the style and content of the Hardboiled school was gradually refined to be as close as possible to Hammett's example. The writers found the wisecracking street slang that existed in the alleyways and gutters of America, then combined these words with tight plots and crusading heroes, to craft violent, moral, asexual stories which had a veneer of reality. The restrained 'realism' cloaked a multitude of detectives, criminals and grifters in their sometimes unbelievable, and mostly salacious adventures. The more literary American writers of the time, like Ernest Hemingway (*A Farewell to Arms* (1929)), William Faulkner (*Sanctuary* (1931)), and John O'Hara (*Appointment in Samarra* (1934)), also began using the American language popularised by the Hardboiled writers. Dashiell Hammett (1894-1961), a former Pinkerton detective – he knew a man who stole a Ferris wheel – created the Continental Op and Sam Spade who appeared in the novels *Red Harvest* (1929) and *The Maltese Falcon* (1930) respectively. The frightening thing about these 'heroes' is that they were detached observers of people with money and power. Their emotions seemed to have little effect on their intellectual actions. They were cold people who acted as judge, jury and executioner.

There are many other tough *Black Mask* writers who followed Hammett's tradition, including Paul Cain (1902-1966) (*Fast One* (1933), *Seven Slayers* (1946)), and Raoul Whitfield (1898-1945) (*Green Ice* (1930), *Death In A Bowl* (1932)). However, Raymond Chandler (1888-1959) was the writer who changed the Hardboiled protagonist, and most influenced all subsequent Hardboiled writers. Chandler came to crime writing late in life but he brought a lyrical approach to the genre which served to romanticise the tough 'tecs, especially his own Philip Marlowe (*The Big Sleep* (1939)). His literary embellishments served to move the reader one more step away from the terror that is death, murder and betrayal. He also refined the wisecracking voice which became the model upon which 1,000 private eyes have been launched. At the time, and for many years, these authors were known as Tough Guy or Hardboiled writers. (There was even a *Hardboiled* magazine which ran for five issues from October 1936 to February 1937.) Hardboiled has become the most common description. However, I intend to show that there is another literature which is present within some Hardboiled stories, and is also running parallel with it. This is Noir Fiction.

The history of the word Noir is not as straightforward as you might expect. Noir is a French word which means the colour black, and can express the gloom and sorrow of mourning. Noir became known internationally through the game of Roulette where it appears on the table opposite Rouge (Red). In the game, they are the only colours upon which you could bet, which gave you a 50% chance of winning, and a 50% chance to lose. (A Noir Fiction book uses this idea in its title: *You Play the Black and the Red Comes Up* (1938) by Richard Hallas (aka Eric Knight).) Even then, all is not what it seems because the wheel also contains the numbers 0 and 00, which means that the odds are stacked against you even more. Gamblers know that Roulette is a suckers game because there is no skill involved – it is all down to pure luck. The only reason to play Roulette is if you want to lose. The French coined the phrase Roman Noir (Black Novel) to describe the Gothic or Terror novels which first appeared in the second half of the 18th century in England. These were novels or stories about the dark side of life. They mixed several aesthetic influences (the sentimental, the sublime, rococo, sepulchral poetry), different tastes (attraction for the past, the gothic style, a change of scenery) and gave nature a sense of waste and desolation. Often supernatural and moral elements were added to allow the author to describe excess and frenzy, and to write stories which demonstrate the power and vanity of evil, of misery and the victory of innocence. The Gothic novel, through the use of the supernatural and the fantastic, is a perversion of the aesthetics of the Sublime, being obsessed with confinement and presenting the past as a pathological determination. (The concept of the Sublime was put forward in 1674. There the emphasis in writing (mainly poetry and essays since the novel form was then in its infancy) was on obscurity, power, darkness, solitude and vastness. Nature was the source of the Sublime. Most Noir Fictions of the 20th century are decidedly anti-nature since they are set almost exclusively within the city.)

The first Gothic novel was *The Castle of Otranto* (1764) by Horace Walpole, which begins with the death of a groom during his wedding and escalates into supernatural tale featuring mistaken identity and doomed lovers. (Anybody familiar with the work of 20th century writer Cornell Woolrich will recognise these themes within his work.) This type of novel became known as a Gothic novel because they were usually set in a medieval castle, convent, monastery or an ancient building. In fact, the titles often referred to a tomb, a castle, a convent, a secret passage or a forest. However, this origin was soon forgotten and Gothic came to represent 'the horror within'. Roman Noir told of the misfortunes of virtue and the havoc wrought by love, and contrasted these against a background of order and morality (as represented by the setting). The conventions of the Roman Noir (playing with extreme feelings, mixture of eroticism, religious references and satanism), its geography and space (foreign countries, castles, cellars, secret passages), its often naïve usage of references to the supernatural, and its emphasis on horror have meant that the genre has been associated with a literature of rupture and subversion. The Roman Noir investigates the past of its characters to determine what horrific experiences they underwent to pervert their moral character. Thus, just as the orderly settings (castle) reveal their chaos when looked at in detail (dungeon, secret passages), so do the characters. As an extension of this, it reveals the chaotic/unpredictable beast/

barbarian within an orderly society. However, to reveal this to the audience, the author must adopt an unrealistic writing form. As early as the 18th century, the Roman Noir was used to deal with social taboos through comparison of the present and the past, morality and immorality, open space and confinement, reality and unreality. Despite the conventional conclusions of most of the early Gothic novels, the terror element remained an integral part of it – the idea was not to show the world as completely evil but to create doubt about the future because the world contains both good and evil. Examples of English writers of the Roman Noir include Mrs Ann Radcliffe (she was greatly imitated in France), Mary Shelley (*Frankenstein* (1818)), Wilkie Collins and Sheridan Le Fanu. French writers include Abbot Prévost, Vicomte d'Arlincourt (*Le Solitaire*), Victor Hugo (*Han d'Islande*) and Théophile Gautier (*La Morte Amoureuse*). American Gothic writers include Charles Brockden Brown, Nathaniel Hawthorne and Edgar Allan Poe.

In the 1930s, French publisher Gallimard had translated some of the emerging American writers including William Faulkner, James M Cain, Horace McCoy and Erskine Caldwell. They were very popular with readers, as well as with the leading French writers of the time. With the end of World War Two, Gallimard decided to launch a new imprint to publish the English and American Hardboiled novels they could not publish during the war. In August 1945, Série Noire was born under Marcel Duhamel's editorship. As well as meaning The Black Series the name was also a play on words because 'une série noire' literally means a succession of bad events. The first two titles were by Peter Cheyney, a British writer who emulated the American Hardboiled style. Cheyney and another Britisher, James Hadley Chase, had 12 titles between them in the first 30. The rest of the list was taken up by Raymond Chandler, Horace McCoy, W R Burnett, Dashiell Hammett and others. A success from the beginning because it mixed the successful Hardboiled with the gloomier 'maudit' (cursed, wretched) literature of Jim Thompson, David Goodis and others, and each new title was assured of a first print run of 30,000 copies. The series became a staple of French literature and is soon to reach book number 2500. Within the English language, the only use of Noir has been in Film Noir, to describe atmospheric crime films released from 1939 to 1958. (Film Noir was coined by French critic Nino Frank in 1946, but only came into common English usage in the early 1970s.) Noir began to be used within crime fiction in 1983, when Nick Kimberley used 'noir' and 'maudit' to describe Jim Thompson's work in the introduction to the Black Box Thriller collection of 4 Jim Thompson novels. Then in 1984, Barry Gifford used the term Roman Noir in his introductions to the Black Lizard reprints of Jim Thompson's novels. Since then, Noir has been stuck onto the cover blurbs of many novels, although nobody seems to know what it means.

Paul Duncan

Noir Fiction by Paul Duncan is published by Pocket Essentials at £3.99

CLASSIC CRIME COVERS
AN OCCASIONAL SERIES

SIMENON'S RED LIGHTS

As a taster for our forthcoming Georges Simenon issue, here's an extract (the first chapter) from the much-anticipated No Exit Press issue of his classic Red Lights*…*

He called it 'going into the tunnel', an expression of his own, for his private use, which he never used in talking to anyone else, least of all to his wife. He knew exactly what it meant, and what it was like to be in the tunnel; yet, curiously, when he was there he never allowed himself to admit the fact, except for occasional brief instants, and always too late. As for determining the precise moment when he entered it, he had often tried to do this afterwards, but never with success.

Today, for example, he had started Labour Day weekend in the best of spirits. The same thing had happened on other occasions. It had also happened that the weekend had nevertheless finished badly. But there was no reason why this should be inevitable.

He left his office on Madison Avenue at five o'clock, and three minutes later had joined his wife at their little bar on Forty-Fifth Street, where she had arrived first and had ordered a martini without waiting for him. There were not many regular customers in the dimly lighted room. In fact he did not see a single face he knew, because everyone was rushing, even more hurriedly than on other Fridays, for the cars and trains which would take them to the sea or into the country. Within an hour New York would be empty except, in the quiet districts, for men in their shirtsleeves and barelegged women seated in their doorways.

It was not yet raining. Since first thing that morning, and indeed for the past three days, the sky had been overcast, the air so laden with moisture that one could gaze steadily at the yellow splash of the sun as though looking at it through a pane of frosted glass. The weather forecasts were now predicting local storms and holding out hopes of a cooler night.

'Tired?'

'Not very.'

They met there at the same time every evening in the summer, when the children were away in camp, always sitting on the same stools, and Louis, the barman, would greet them with a wink and start mixing their drinks without waiting for the order. They felt no need to start talking at once. One would offer the other a cigarette. Sometimes Nancy would push the dish of peanuts towards him, or he would pass her the olives, while they gazed absently at the small, pallid rectangle of the television receiver set high in the right-hand corner of the bar. Images flickered across it. A voice poured out a commentary on a baseball game, or a woman sang. It was quite unimportant.

'You'll be able to take a shower before we start.'

It was her way of looking after him. She never failed to ask if he was tired, darting at him the sort of look one gives a delicate child or one that seems to be sickening for something. It ruffled him slightly. He knew he did not look his best at that time, with his shirt sticking to his body and his beard beginning to show, seeming darker against the skin softened by the heat. She was bound to have noticed the damp circles under his armpits.

It was the more irritating since she herself was as fresh as she had been when she left the house that morning, without a crease in her lightly starched linen suit, so that no one would have supposed, from the look of her, that she had spent the day in an office. She might have been taken for one of those women who don't get up before four in the afternoon, and make their first appearance at cocktail-time.

Louis asked:

'You going to get the kids?'

Steve nodded.

'New Hampshire?'

'Maine.'

How many parents were there, in New York and the suburbs, who that evening would be setting off along the roads to fetch their children home from the camps up North? A hundred thousand? Two hundred thousand? Probably more. The figure must be tucked away in some corner of the newspaper. And then there were the children who had spent the summer with an aunt or grandmother in the country or by the sea. And it was the same everywhere, from one seaboard to the other, from the Canadian frontier right down to Mexico.

From the television screen a man in shirt-sleeves, wearing thickly rimmed glasses which seemed to make him feel hot, announced in a tone of gloomy conviction:

'The National Safety Council predicts that this evening between forty and forty-five million motorists will be on the roads, and it estimates that between now and Monday evening four hundred and thirty-five people will have lost their lives in road accidents.'

He finished lugubriously, before making way for a beer advertisement:

'Don't be one of them. Drive carefully.'

Why four hundred and thirty-five, and not four hundred and thirty or four hundred and forty? Sandwiched between the regular programmes, these predictions would be repeated all that night, and tomorrow and the next day, until towards the end they acquired the suspense of a race-commentary. Steve recalled the voice of a speaker last year, when they were bringing the children back from Maine on the Sunday evening:

'Up to now the number of deaths is considerably lower than the official forecast, despite the collision of two airliners over Washington airport, in which thirty-two people lost their lives. But watch out! The weekend isn't over yet!'

'Myself' said Louis, talking as usual in an undertone and fetching a fresh supply of peanuts, 'my wife and kid are with my mother-in-law, near Quebec. They're coming back by train tomorrow.'

Had Steve meant to order another martini? As a rule Nancy and he had only one, except occasionally when they dined in town before going to the theatre.

Perhaps he had wanted to, not necessarily to give himself a lift or because of the heat. In fact, for no special reason. Or rather, because this was not an ordinary weekend. When they got back from Maine there would be no more thought of summer, or of vacations; it would be winter setting in, the days growing shorter and the children at home, obliging them to come straight back from the office; a more complicated life altogether, without any let-up.

Didn't that rate another drink? He had not said anything, had made no movement, no sign to Louis. But Nancy guessed what was in his mind, and at once slipped down from her stool.

'You'd better pay. It's time we were going.'

He wasn't really angry about it. A bit disappointed perhaps, slightly put out. What did irritate him was that Louis had known perfectly well what was going on.

They had to cross two streets to reach the car-park where they left their car for the day, and once past Third Avenue one might have thought it was a Sunday.

'Do you want me to drive?' said Nancy.

He said no, took his place at the wheel, drove towards Queensboro Bridge where the procession of cars was moving at a snail's pace. Two hundred yards further on a car had already turned over at the edge of the sidewalk, and a woman was seated on the ground with people crowding round her and a policeman trying to keep traffic moving along until the arrival of an ambulance.

'There's no point in leaving too soon,' said Nancy, feeling in her handbag for cigarettes. 'In an hour or two the worst of the crush will be over.'

A few drops rolled down the windscreen as they drove through Brooklyn, but the rain which had been forecast had not yet really started.

He was in a good mood at that moment, and still was when they reached their home in Scottville, a new building-lot in the middle of Long Island.

'Do you mind if we just have something cold?'

'I'd prefer it.'

The house, too, would be different once the children were back. During the summer he always had a feeling of aimlessness, as though the two of them had no reason for being there, or for being in one room more than another, and they were constantly at a loss to know what to do with their evenings.

'While you're making sandwiches I'll slip out and get some cigarettes.'

'There are some in the cupboard.'

'Well, it'll save time if I fill up with gas and oil.'

She made no objection to this, which surprised him. And he did in fact go to the garage. While they were checking the tyres he darted into the Italian restaurant to have a whisky at the bar.

'Scotch?'

'Rye.'

Yet he didn't really like rye. He had chosen the stronger of the two because he would probably not have another chance of a drink that night, and they'd be driving for hours along the highway.

Could one say that he had entered the

tunnel? He had had only two drinks, no more than when they went to the theatre and Nancy drank the same as he did...

'Did you get cigarettes?'

'You said there were some in the cupboard. I filled up with gas and had the tyres checked.'

'We'll get some as we go.'

There weren't any cigarettes in the house. Either she had made a mistake or she had deliberately told him otherwise.

She stopped him as he was on his way to the bathroom.

'You can have your shower after we've eaten, while I'm stacking the dishes.'

She didn't order him about, actually, but she arranged their life in her own way, as though it were the natural thing to do. He was wrong. He knew he was wrong. Whenever he had had a drink or two he saw her differently, becoming annoyed by things which ordinarily he took for granted.

'You'd better take your tweed jacket and your rain coat.'

A breeze was getting up outside, stirring the leaves of the still-slender trees which had been planted five years before, when the houses had been built and the streets laid out. Some had never taken root, and two or three attempts to replace them had been equally fruitless. Across the way one of their neighbours was attaching a trailer with a canoe on it to his car, while his wife, flushed with recent sunburn, her fat thighs filling pale blue shorts, stood at the edge of the sidewalk holding the fishing-rods.

'What are you thinking about?'

'Nothing special.'

'I wonder if Dana's grown any more. Last month I thought he was taller, and his legs looked thinner.'

'It's normal at his age.'

Nothing special happened. He had his shower, got dressed, and then his wife reminded him to go and switch off the electricity meter in the garage while she went round to see that all the windows were closed.

'Shall I take the bags?'

'Make sure they're properly shut.'

Despite the breeze and the lowering sky, his clean shirt was damp by the time he got in behind the wheel.

'Shall we go the same way as last time?'

'We swore we'd never go that way again.'

'Just the same, it's the best.'

Less than a quarter of an hour later they were wedged in among thousands of other cars moving in the same direction, with inexplicable hold-ups and occasional, momentary bursts of almost frantic speed.

It was at the beginning of Merrit Parkway that they ran into their first thunderstorm, when darkness had not quite fallen and the cars had only switched on their sidelights. There were three lanes of traffic between the white lines heading north but many fewer, of course, coming the opposite way, and one could hear the rain drumming on the steel roofs, the monotonous swish of the wheels throwing up a spray of water, the irritating sweep-sweep of the windscreen wiper.

'Sure you aren't tired?'

'Certain.'

Sometimes one file got ahead of the others and some times one had a sense of losing ground.

'You should have gotten into the third line.'

'I'm trying.'

'Not now. There's a fool behind us.'

At every lightning-flash one had a glimpse of faces in the darkened interiors of the adjacent cars, all with the same strained expression.

'Cigarette?'

'Thanks, I'd like one.'

She always passed them to him lighted when he was driving.

'Like the radio on?'

'I don't mind.'

But she had to switch it off again because of the static caused by the storm.

It was not worth the effort of talking, either. The constant hubbub made it necessary to raise one's voice, which soon became tiring. Gazing straight ahead he had a sidelong vision of Nancy's profile, palely shining in the half-light, and he asked her several times:

'What are you thinking about?'

'Nothing special.'

Once she added:

'And you?' He said:

'About the children.'

It was not true. In fact he was not thinking about anything special either. To be precise, he was sorry he had managed to slide into the third traffic-lane, because it would be difficult to change without his wife asking why. Yet in a little while, when they had left the Parkway, there would be bars along the side of the road.

Had they ever driven the children to or from camp without his pulling in a few times for a drink? Only once, three years ago, when he had had a terrible scene with Nancy the night before, and, both deeply shaken, they had made the weekend into a second honeymoon.

'We seem to have left the storm behind.'

She switched off the windscreen wiper, but had to switch it on again for a few minutes because big, isolated drops continued to splash against the screen.

'You're not cold?'

'No.'

The air had grown cool. With one elbow thrust out of the window, Steve could feel the wind blowing under his shirtsleeve.

'And you?'

'Not yet. I'll put on my coat in a little while.'

Why did they feel an obscure need to exchange remarks of this sort? Was it to reassure themselves? If so, what were they afraid of?

'Now the storm's over I'll try the radio again.'

There was music. Nancy gave him another cigarette, and lighting one herself lay back on her seat, blowing the smoke above her head.

'Special report of the Connecticut Automobile Club...'

They were already in Connecticut, fifty miles from New London.

'Labour Day weekend claimed its first victim in Connecticut at 7.45 this evening, when at the intersection of Highways 1 and 118, at Darrien, a private car driven by Mr. MacKillian, of New York, collided with a truck driven by Robert Ostling. MacKillian and his passenger, John Roe, were killed instantly. The truck driver was uninjured. Ten minutes later, thirty miles from there, a car driven by...'

He switched off. His wife opened her mouth to say something and then stopped. Had she noticed that, perhaps unconsciously, he had slowed down a little?

She finally said:

'Past Providence there'll be less traffic.'

'Until we run into the Boston mob.'

He was not shaken by the accident reports, not alarmed. What got on his nerves was the incessant hum of wheels on either side of him, the headlights rushing to meet him every hundred yards, and also the sensation of being caught in a tide, with no way of escaping either to right or to left or even of driving more slowly, because his mirror showed a triple-string of lights following bumper to bumper behind him.

Neon signs had begun to flash by on the right, where, with the gasoline-pumps, they were the only manifestation of life. Except for them one might have thought that the highroad was suspended in space, and that nothing existed beyond it but night and silence. The towns, the villages, were set further back, and only rarely did a vague, reddish glow in the sky give a hint of their existence.

The only immediate reality was that of the restaurants and bars which sprang out of the darkness every few miles, their signs advertising in red, green, and blue letters brands of beer or whisky.

He was now in the second traffic-lane. He had edged gradually into it without his wife's noticing, and suddenly, seeing a gap, he slid into the first.

'What are you doing?'

He nearly overshot a bar whose neon sign announced, 'The Little Cottage', braked just in time, so abruptly that the car behind had to make a sudden swerve and a flood of abuse poured from it. The driver even shook his fist out of the window.

'I have to go to the men's room,' he said, keeping his voice as natural as possible while he pulled up at the side of the road. 'You aren't thirsty?'

No.

It often happened. She would wait for him in the car.

In another car parked in front of the bar, a couple were so closely embraced that for a moment he wondered whether they were one person or two.

A moment later, pushing open the door, he felt a different man, and he paused for an instant to survey the room bathed in a dim orange light. This bar was like all the others along the road, and not so very different from Louis' place on Forty-Fifth Street, with the same television set in the corner, the same smells, the same lights.

'Dry martini with lemon peel,' he said as the barman turned to him.

'Single?'

'Double.'

If he hadn't been asked he would have made do with a single, but a double was better, because his wife probably wouldn't allow him to stop again.

He hesitated, glancing towards the door of the toilet, and then dutifully started for it from a sort of honesty, passing a man with very dark hair who was telephoning with a hand curved round the side of his mouth. His voice was harsh.

'Yes. Just tell him what I told you. Nothing else. He'll understand. I tell you, he'll understand, see?'

Steve would have liked to hear more, but the man glanced at him as he spoke with a far from encouraging look. What was it all about? Who was at the other end of the line?

He came back to the bar and emptied his glass in two gulps, feeling in his pocket for the money. Would Nancy hold her tongue? Wasn't it bad enough that just because of her he couldn't stay there a few minutes simply to look at people and relax his nerves?

Perhaps he had now entered the tunnel. Perhaps he had been in it ever since they left Long Island. If so, he was not aware of the fact and thought himself the most normal man on earth, not in the least affected by the one or two drinks he had had.

Why did he feel uncomfortable, even guilty, as he went towards the car and got in without looking at his wife? She asked no questions, made no comment.

'That's better!' he murmured as though to himself, starting the engine.

It seemed to him now that there were fewer cars on the road, that the pace had slackened, so much so that he passed three or four that were really going too slowly. An ambulance coming the other way left him unmoved, his attention being occupied at that moment by strange lights, then by a white barrier which suddenly loomed in front of them.

'Detour,' said Nancy's calm voice, a little too expressionless.

'I can see.'

'On the left.'

This made him blush, because he had nearly turned right.

He grumbled:

'We've never once come this way without having to turn off somewhere. Why can't they repair the road in winter?'

'In the snow?' she asked, in the same voice.

'Well, in the fall – anyway, some time when there aren't forty million motorists on the roads.'

'You've passed the intersection.'

'What intersection?'

'The one marked with an arrow showing the way back to the Highway?'

'What about the people behind us?' he asked sarcastically.

There were still cars following, fewer than there had been, however.

'Everybody isn't going to Maine.'

'Don't you worry. I'll get you to Maine all right.' A moment later he seemed to have triumphed, because they were emerging onto a major road.

'Well? What about your arrow now?'

'This isn't Highway Number One.'

'We'll soon know.'

What set his nerves on edge was her self-confidence, the calm with which she answered him.

He persisted:

'I suppose you can't be wrong, can you?'

She said nothing, and this irritated him still more.

'Go on! Say what you want to say!'

'Do you remember the time when we made a detour of sixty miles?'

'And dodged the worst of the traffic!'

'But without meaning to!'

'Listen, Nancy, if you want to start a quarrel why not say so?'

'I'm not trying to quarrel. I'm trying to find out where we are.'

'Well, as I'm driving, do me a favour and don't fuss!'

She remained silent. He did not recognize the road, either. It was narrower and not so good, without a single filling-station since they had entered it; and another storm was rumbling in the sky.

Nancy quietly took the road-map out of the glove compartment and switched on the light on the dash board.

'We must be between One and Eighty-two, on a road going to Norwich, but I can't find the number.'

She tried, too late, to catch the name of a village that sprang up out of the darkness and then they had left its few lights behind and were passing through woods.

'Don't you really think we should turn back?'

'No.'

With the map still on her knees she lit a cigarette, without offering him one.

'Furious?' he said.

'Me?'

'Yes, you! Why not admit you're furious? Just because I happened to miss the highway and we have to go a few extra miles! I seem to remember that not long ago you were saying we had any amount of time.'

'Watch out!'

'What for?'

'You nearly went off the road.'

'So now I don't know how to drive?'

'I didn't say that.'

And then the words burst from him, for no precise reason.

'No, you didn't say it, but now I'm going to say something, my pet, and you might as well get it into your head, once and for all... '

The strangest thing was that he had no notion what he was going to say. He groped round for something strong, decisive; something to give his wife a good dose of the humility she so badly needed.

'You see, Nancy, maybe you're the only person who doesn't know it, but you're a pest!'

'Watch the road, will you!'

'Sure I'll watch the road! And I'll drive nice and carefully, so as not to go off the tracks. Do you know what tracks I'm talking about?'

It seemed to him extremely subtle, and dazzling in its truth. Almost as though he had made a new discovery. What was wrong with Nancy, finally, was that she always stayed on the rails, never allowed herself the least diversion.

'You don't understand, do you?'

'Do I have to?'

'What? Do you have to know what I think? God almighty, it might at least help you to try and understand other people and make life a bit more pleasant for them. For me, in particular. Only I doubt if you care.'

'Wouldn't you let me drive?'

'No, I wouldn't. Just for the sake of argument, suppose instead of always thinking of yourself and being so darned sure you're right, you took a good look at yourself in the mirror and asked yourself...'

He was laboriously struggling to express something he felt, which he was convinced he had felt every day of his life throughout the eleven years they had been married. It was not the first time it had happened, but now he was sure he had made a discovery which would enable him to explain everything. She would have to understand some time, wouldn't she? And the day she understood, maybe she'd try and treat him like a grown man.

'Can you think of anything more senseless than to be like a train, always following the same route? Along the same tracks? Well, just now on the Parkway I had the feeling I was like a train. Other cars were pulling up and men were getting out without having to ask anyone's leave to go and have a glass of beer.'

'Did you have a beer?'

He hesitated, decided upon frankness.

'No.'

'A martini?'

'Yes.'

'A double?'

It infuriated him to have to answer:

'Yes.'

'And before that?' She was unkind enough to insist.

'Before what?'

'Before we left.'

'I don't understand.'

'What did you drink when you went to fill up with gas?'

This time he lied.

'Nothing.'

'Oh?'

'You don't believe me?'

'If it's true, a double martini hit you harder than usual.'

'You think I'm drunk?'

'You're certainly talking the way you do when you've been drinking.'

'Meaning, I'm not making sense?'

'I don't know if it's sense or not, but I know you hate me.'

'Why won't you try to understand?'

'Understand what?'

'That I don't hate you, that I love you, in fact, that I'd be perfectly happy with you if only you'd treat me as a grown man.'

'By letting you drink at every bar along the way?'

'You see!'

'What am I supposed to see?'

'You have to put it in the most humiliating way you can. You deliberately exaggerate everything. Am I a drunk?'

'Of course not. I'd never have married a drunk.'

'Do I often have too much?'

'Not very.'

'Not even once a month. Perhaps once in three months.'

'Well then, what's the matter with you?'

'There wouldn't be anything the matter with me if you didn't treat me like a worm. Just because for one evening I'd like to get a little outside everyday life!'

'Does it cramp you so much?'

'I didn't say that. You take Dick, for instance. I don't suppose he ever goes to bed less than half-tight. But that doesn't stop you thinking how interesting he is, and you talk seriously to him by the hour, even when he's been drinking.'

'For one thing, he isn't my husband.'

'And what else?'

'There's a truck ahead of us.'

'I can see.'

'Be quiet a minute. We're coming to a cross-road and I want to see what's on the road-sign.'

'You don't like me talking about Dick?'

'I don't mind.'

'You're sorry you didn't marry him instead of me?'

'No.'

They were again on the highway, with two lines of cars travelling very much faster than in the outskirts of New York, and overtaking furiously. Perhaps in the hope of silencing him, Nancy switched on the radio, which was giving out the eleven o'clock news.

'The police have reason to believe that Sid Halligan, who escaped last night from Sing-Sing Penitentiary, and has so far evaded his pursuers – '

She turned it off again.

'Why did you switch off?'

'I didn't think you were interested.'

He wasn't interested. He had never heard of Sid Halligan, did not even know that a prisoner had escaped from Sing-Sing the night before. He had merely thought, as he heard the words, of the man telephoning in the bar, with his hand cupped round his mouth and a fierce glare in his eyes. There was nothing to it, except for her switching off without asking him, but it is trifles such as these...

Where had they got to when she had broken off the argument? They had been talking about Dick Lowell, who had married a friend of Nancy's, and with whom they sometimes spent an evening.

Hell, what was the good of arguing? Did Dick care what his wife thought? The mistake he made was that he was always worrying about what Nancy thought, and always trying to win her approval.

'What are you doing?'

'Stopping, that's what.'

'Listen...'

This bar had a shabby look, with nothing but a few half-broken-down cars outside, and that made him all the more anxious to go in.

'If you stop,' Nancy was saying, carefully pronouncing each syllable, 'I warn you I shall go on alone.'

It gave him a shock. For an instant he stared at her incredulously, and she met his gaze steadily. She was as trim and neat as when they had left New York – cool as a cucumber, he thought.

Perhaps nothing would have happened and he would have given way, if she had not added:

'You can always come on to the camp by bus.'

He felt his lip twist in a queer sort of smile and, as calm as she was herself, he reached for the ignition key, which he took out and put in his pocket.

Nothing of the kind had ever happened to them before. He could not turn back now. He was convinced that she needed a lesson.

He got out of the car and shut the door without looking at her, and made himself walk with a steady stride towards the entrance of the bar. When he looked round from the doorway she had not moved and he could see her pale profile through the glass.

He went in. Faces turned towards him, transformed by the smoke as though in the trick-mirrors at a fair, and when he put his hand on the counter he felt it sticky with alcohol.

Red Lights is published by No Exit Press

THAT OL' GANG OF MINE...

*Film reviews with **Michael Carlson***

Gangs of New York (directed by Martin Scorsese)
Catch Me If You Can (directed by Steven Spielberg)

The frustrating thing about *Gangs of New York* is one can see very easily what the film might have been, but you never feel that Scorsese's original four-hour cut would've been very different – only bigger, longer, with more set pieces, and it's the set pieces which Scorsese does so well in this one. *Gangs of New York* is an epic film clawing to escape the skin of a much smaller effort, like one of those insects with eggs laid in its belly. Those eggs have hatched into Leonardo DiCaprio, Daniel Day Lewis and Cameron Diaz, and they've eaten the big bug from the inside. This isn't *Cleopatra,* where the epic overkill existed merely to gloss the leads. Nor is it *Heaven's Gate,* where a director's epic indulgence subsumed both story and stars. It's more like Peckinpah's *Major Dundee,* where the cut version focuses a story that wants to sprawl into one of romantic competition between its leads, and I admit it isn't a very good analogy because I can only guess what the original cut of *Major Dundee* looked like. Of course *Gangs* 'director's cut' is probably ready on DVD already. But here one thinks of Leone's *Once Upon A Time In America*, badly served by the producers' original cutting. Though they said they cut as much for coherence as for time, the cuts simply revealed the complexities of the film Leone conceived. Such isn't the case here. *Gangs of New York* contains some bravura film-making, particularly when Scorsese illuminates his vision of mid 19th century New York's ground-level inferno to the screen. But the film is also a tease, a three-card monte trick, king, queen, and jack: and in this case its Jack is straight from *Titanic,* another epic which existed merely to provide a special effects disaster behind a love story. Scorsese would rather we saw his model as Fellini's *Satyricon*, as the bravura Cinecittà sets remind us, but the Cameronisation of the film is hard to miss. Leonardo DiCaprio seems to see his character as something out of *Mean Streets: The Prequel*, but can't avoid playing beefcake á la *Titanic II: Jack Grows Up.* I was half expecting Cameron Diaz to actually make it to her getaway ship and then collide with an iceberg before it cleared the Narrows. "Amsterdam!", "Jenny!", "Amsterdam", glug glug glug… Sadly, it was not to be. Yet *Gangs* is that rare film where the whole is far more than the sum of its parts. What works best is the history: the battling fire companies letting buildings burn while they fight, then robbing the buildings they save. Jim Broadbent as Boss Tweed, negotiating with the 'fine' families that really run New York (Broadbent, by the way, reinforced my theory that British actors turn in two performances at a time by playing Tweed as a character from *Topsy Turvy*). The settings, at least until we get uptown, convey a real sense of the chaos that was New York, with extensive bows to the cinema of 18th century ribaldry, à la *Tom Jones*. Yet the characters are constantly undermining the settings. The rumble scenes are involving if overdone, like Hollywood gunfights, but someone should have told Cara Seymour that Hell-Cat Maggie is not a dancer from *Cats*. Watching the Dead Rabbits prepare for their opening brawl, I flashed back to the commentary box watching Oakland Raider fans dressing up for an American football contest. Then I waited for Maggie to burst into 'We Are Siamese If You Please'. Daniel Day-Lewis' performance is full of over the top bravado, and great Brando-ish *Waterfront* vowels, but cartoon villains like Snidley Whiplash or Dudley Nightshade would be embarrassed at the moustache-twirling hamming. It works because it's set against DiCaprio's little league De Niro, all pouting and furrowing of brow. Maybe he was trying to figure out exactly what sort of deal he'd worked with the Chinamen: that's one plot point that must've been edited out. Maybe the original ending had DiCaprio in an opium den, giving a De Niro smile to the camera. Instead he pouts, Diaz frowns, they fall in love. Diaz is all over the place: we never get a sense of what it is about Amsterdam that appeals to her, apart from the fact he followed her uptown, maybe he understands she's an uptown girl tired of living in a downtown world. I'm still trying to figure out what a black guy is doing in the racist pure-American gangs, or why no one seems to notice he's black until the draft riots begin. The riots themselves are another fine historical tableau: it's a shame the characters can't live up to the history into which they've been set. Still, Scorsese's visual flair keeps things moving and despite picking the scenes apart, they held me despite myself. Perhaps it would all work better if Scorsese could have made DiCaprio into Johnny-Boy II. Instead, he's created a brilliant Manhattan, and filled it with the Dead End Kids, only with better weapons. And he's done something no other director could do: turned Leo DiCaprio into Leo Gorcey.

Which is just about where DiCaprio starts, as a kid in New Rochelle, New York, in *Catch Me If You Can*. But since Steven Spielberg is the world's champion director of stories about lost boys, DiCaprio gets far more of a chance to move beyond Gorcey: this may be his most affecting performance since *Gilbert Grape*. It's a killer homage: early 1960s-style credits in homage to Saul Bass, John Williams score restrained in imitation of the MJQ. It's playful in its evocation of the early Sixties and brilliant in the way Spielberg and photographer Janusz Kaminski frame DiCaprio in various distorted backgrounds: trapping him in tiny rooms and losing him in vast crowds. But once DiCaprio, as con-man and forger Frank Abagnale, gets into gear, the story starts an arc in which the fun gets progressively less and less, and Frank's need for a surrogate family grows more and more. All Spielberg's films address this issue, all of them share a Disneyesque concern with what George Bush would call the 'nucular family', and Frank Senior's (Christopher Walken in a stunning performance) failure to hold together his family is the real centre of this film. This also makes for an awkward transition for Tom Hanks, as the plodding FBI agent who eventually captures Frank, and becomes his father figure. It's hard to criticise Spielberg for this plot twist, because it's true, but despite its predictability it is also undercut by the failures not only of Frank's family but also that of Nurse Strong, to whom Frank seems drawn only after he learns she's been abandoned by her parents for having an abortion. Spielberg also gets to portray the French police and prisons the same way Alan Parker did the Turks 25 years ago: it's a subtle indication of who the bad guys are nowadays. Still, this is as close as Steve has come yet to a full Mickey Mouse Club Spin and Marty picture of the universe, and DiCaprio gets to leave Leo Gorcey behind, and emerge as a teenage Sean Connery in the process.

THE BIG ROUND-UP

*Books on Film with **Michael Carlson***

The Conversations: Walter Murch and the Art of Editing Film by Michael Ondaatje (Bloomsbury, £25.00, 0747557748)

The New Biographical Dictionary of Film by David Thomson (Little, Brown, £25.00, 0316859052)

Silent Stars by Jeanine Basinger (Wesleyan University Press, £19.50, 0819564516)

You Ain't Heard Nothin' Yet by Andrew Sarris (Oxford University Press, £13.99, 0195134265)

Hollywood in Crisis: Cinema and American Society 1929-1939 by Colin Shindler (Routledge, £18.99, 0415103142)

Vertigo by Charles Barr (BFI Film Classics, £8.99, 0851709184)

Conversations is one of the most fascinating books of any sort which it's been my pleasure to read. Having interviewed both Ondaatje (years ago) and Murch (for CT27), and seen a live version of their conversation in the West End, I was prepared, but the words on the page are even more impressive. Murch's polyglot intellect combines with a very practical sense of craft, something which Ondaatje echoes in a much narrower, but perhaps more intuitive way. The combination is striking, and even though sometimes the book is best when Murch is simply telling a story, say about the problems of the French scene in *Apocalypse Now,* there are other times when

Ondaatje's sensibility opens the reader's eyes as well, and not just when they are discussing the adaptation of *The English Patient.* I think Murch may well be best on Orson Welles, for Welles had that same kind of mix of intellect and craft which movies, at their best, demand, but lacked the willingness to sit down and get the boring bits done that Murch seems to relish. Yet Welles could write a monster memo about what was wrong with the studio re-edit of *Touch of Evil*, almost shot by shot, improving it and being very politic in how his improvements were suggested. One gets the sense that the role Murch enjoyed playing for Welles was one he'd already rehearsed with Francis Coppolla, and it's one he relishes. This is a must-have book. I've referenced David Thomson's *Biographical Dictionary* with gratitude on any number of writing occasions. But this latest edition (receiving the particular promotion from '*A*' to '*The*' in its title) seems far less

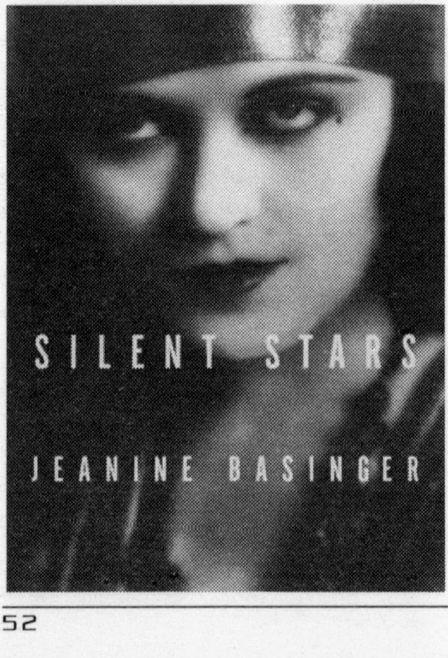

useful. Part of this is understandable, as Thomson has said what he wants to say already, so updating many of the entries seems to consist largely of adding to the filmographies (which are not by any means definitive). This means too many entries drift off into 'then he did this and then he did this…'. But it's also different because times, tastes and Thomson all have changed, not necessarily for the better, since the last edition. A sharp edge seems to be blunted, as if Thomson has adjusted his critical standards to not only the blockbuster, actor-driven films of the 1990s, but to the more flippant, celebrity-driven criticism as well. I don't say this cynically, because I suspect the process has been a natural one, but the other big difference now is Thomson seems more in love with his writing for its own sake. Perhaps he's been reading Anthony Lane in the New Yorker, or perhaps he takes seriously the built-in awe with which Americans regard British journalists. But too much of this edition replaces sharp insights with sharp prose. I'd suggest at least paging through the 1981 or 1994 books, in a library or second-hand (if you're lucky enough to find one) before you spring for the 21st century version. One of the few writers Thomson credits (though not every time he borrows an insight from her) is Janine Basinger, whose *Silent Stars*, first published in 1999, I've finally caught up with. It's a brilliant book, because it explains the silent cinema in the terms of its own era, so we can understand exactly what the contemporary audience (and, indeed, film-makers) saw in Mary Pickford, William S Hart, Marion Davies, or Rin Tin Tin, among others. It's a useful book because, frankly, few of us are likely to be able to see a fraction of the original films which Basinger has watched, but its also valuable because the temptation to judge the silents by contemporary standards is hard to avoid. Basinger skips some of the big names, the Chaplins, Keatons, Lloyds and Gishes for example, because they've been well covered elsewhere. She also skips some figures, especially Wallace Reid, Harry Carey, Ben Turpin, or Blanche Sweet, who might have repaid curiosity. But this book is the closest thing I can think of to making repeated trips to the silent movies, or, as I was fortunate enough to do a quarter of a century ago, compare notes on silent films with my grandfather, who seemed to remember every film he'd ever seen. Or at least every actress. Another catch-up book for me was Andrew Sarris', published in 1998. It's basically a history of the first two decades of talking film, and in some ways a nice complement to *Silent Stars*. Or to Sarris' own magnum opus, *The American Cinema*. But its problem is it's really two books in one. The first, and more effective, proceeds through a history of film genres, and then begins to move through directors, into stars and other essay points. As it does it becomes obvious that some of the essay material is reprinted from other sources, for example obituaries, and has been stitched together in a very sloppy way. Sarris sometimes digresses into his own personal critical battles, and reminds us how often he's been proven right. He doesn't really need to remind us, however: his writing would do that for us. I'm even later discovering Colin Schindler's *Hollywood in Crisis,* published in 1996, but worth seeking out because it conveys a good sense of what function movies had for American society in the decade from 1929 to 1939, and how the studio business worked in that decade of depression. It's hard to understand, say, Frank Capra's particular blend of despair and schmaltzy hope without understanding the era, and the precarious balance between the studio tycoons with the Roosevelt New Deal. At one point Schindler notices that most of the big gangsters of the 1920s and 30s were second-generation Americans. So too were most of the studio heads... Charles Barr's study of *Vertigo* is really an update of the progress of critical theory, though no less enjoyable a study for that. It's a homage to Robin Wood and Chris Marker, particularly to Wood's suggestion that the film is a dream, an unresolvable fantasy of Hitchcock's madonna/whore dilemma. Certainly, by going back to the changes in the draft screenplays, as documented in Dan Auiler's *Vertigo* (1998), Barr manages to update the 'textual' battle in its most 'oneiric' sense. The eyes have it, as it were.

Michael Carlson

DVD CRIME

Paul McAuley, Barry Forshaw & Kim Newman

Paul McAuley's latest novel is Whole Wide World *(HarperCollins);*
Kim Newman's latest book is Science Fiction/Horror: A Sight and Sound Reader *(BFI).*

The House of Fear
Pursuit to Algiers
Roy William Neill, director/Orbit Media
Ask most Conan Doyle aficionados who gave the definitive acting portrayal of Sherlock Holmes, and the choice usually comes down to one of two men: Basil Rathbone or Jeremy Brett. But Brett had the virtue of high production values, accurate period settings and (best of all) fastidious attention to the original Doyle texts, whereas as Rathbone's incarnation appeared in a series of low-budget Universal B movies, low prestige offerings, most of which ill-advisedly updated the period,

usually to the Second World War. So how is it that the Rathbone films still work incredibly well today? And how can those of us who applaud the authentic, intelligent Watson of Edward Hardwicke still love Nigel Bruce's bumbling idiot in the Universal series? As these two welcome releases attest, there are two factors that make these films still essential viewing: impeccable, authoritative performance from Basil Rathbone as the Master Detective and the highly efficient atmospheric and inventive direction of journeyman filmmaker Roy William Neill. Even in two lesser entries such as *The House of Fear* and *Pursuit to Algiers*, the virtues of these craftsmen shine out gloriously. Unlike earlier issues in the Orbit re-issue series, there are no extras, and with just one movie a disc, they're not exactly great value. But they remain essential viewing for anyone interested in a certain violin-playing cocaine user. A nice touch, too, is the retention of the original period artwork of the sleeves.

The Eye

Pang Brothers, directors/Tartan

Stylish chills from the talented Pang Brothers: a powerfully wrought piece that only suffers from the cynical ploy of going for the youth market by making almost every principal character implausibly young, even experienced doctors and psychologists. Young Mun, who has been blind since childhood, is given an operation to restore her sight, but after receiving a cornea transplant, she starts seeing ghosts everywhere. More disturbingly, when she discovers that the donor was a doomed clairvoyant, it looks increasingly likely that she might share the same tragic fate. The Pang Brothers evoke memories of *The Sixth Sense* and Richard Matheson's *A Stir of Echoes*. The US remake rights are in the hands of Tom Cruise, so expect the customary traducing of the original. DVD extras include a 'Making Of' documentary, a Pang Brothers documentary, and other items.

Rififi

Jules Dassin, director/Fremantle/Arrow

It doesn't date an iota – and, in fact, Dassin's *Du Rififi Chez les Hommes* makes Guy Ritchie and co. look like small beer indeed. Acknowledged as the forerunner of (and the inspiration behind) many modern day crime capers (including *The Usual Suspects* and *Reservoir Dogs),* Jules Dassin's French noir classic remains the quintessential heist movie; this DVD is fully restored with the original French dialogue (anyone who's suffered the dubbed horror that has circulated in the past will be grateful for that).

Evil Dead Trap

Toshiharu Ikeda, director/Artsmagic

This strikingly made Japanese chiller may have a standard plot (mysterious killer decimates a group of hapless individuals in a cloistered environment – in this case, a disused factory), but what grabs the attention is the sheer panache of the filmmaking. Toshiharu Ikeda knows precisely the optimum techniques for unsettling the viewer, and the violent deaths dispatched so operatically here are handled with genuine imagination. Okay, the characters are underdeveloped (and act with all the stupidity we expect from soon-to-be-victims in such situations), but nevertheless *Evil Dead Trap* will guarantee that the viewer is comprehensively gripped throughout its pulse-racing duration. Not, needless to say, for the squeamish.

Legion of the Dead

Olaf Ittenbach, director/Anchor Bay

Olaf Ittenbach is a director of great flair, and this fast-paced piece combines Tarantino-style dialogue and highly creative mayhem. This is crowd-pleasing stuff, but exerts a grip even in a domestic environment.

Hypnosis

Gora Inagaki, director/Artsmagic

A groom kills himself by hanging at his own wedding reception, an elderly man defenestrates himself, and a young track star ends her life by frantic running. What do the three deaths have in common? All three are somehow connected with something called The Green Monkey. Seasoned Detective Sakurai begins to believe that hypnosis is at the basis of the deaths. This is a stylishly made piece; the visuals combine obsessive detail with baroque flourishes. It's clearly a good time for eastern cult cinema.

Barry Forshaw

Insomnia and Insomnia, or, Sleepless in Norway and Alaska

Hollywood remakes of foreign language films do not have a distinguished history. For every success, such as transplanting the plot of *The Seven Samurai* into the Wild West of *The Magnificent Seven,* there are dozens of instances (the transformation of *A Bout de Souffle* into the macho posturing of *Breathless,* say, or *Wings of Desire* into the kitsch sobfest of *City of Angels)* where the heavy hand of Hollywood turns gold into lead. For the process isn't a simple case of substituting American English and American settings; Hollywood also insists on adding familiar stars, and retrofitting quirky originals with industry standard three-act story arcs in which the lead character overcomes adversity and, y'know, *learns* from the experience. But although the first big-budget movie helmed by Christopher Nolan, writer and director of the acclaimed *Memento,* is a remake of the highly original Norwegian thriller *Insomnia,* and was made on a very tight schedule with no opportunity for the usual pre-shoot rehearsals, it's a well-made, entertaining thriller that doesn't succumb to the Curse of the Remake until the very end. For much of the first half of the story, Nolan's version closely follows first-time director Erik Skjoldjærg's original. An experienced but troubled detective is brought into a small town above the Arctic Circle to investigate the murder of a teenage girl whose body was scrubbed clean of anything which might incriminate her killer. The detective sets a trap for the killer, who shoots a cop while making his escape, and in the confusion of a chase through a foggy landscape the detective shoots and kills his partner. With 24/7 daylight playing havoc with his body clock and judgement, the detective tries to cover up his mistake, but then the killer gets in touch; he witnessed what happened, and wants to make a deal. The remake utilises Alaska's scenery, depicted in rich, sombre light by cinematographer Wally Pfister to great effect, adds a brilliantly shot chase across a raft of logs floating down river, and deepens and complicates plot and motivation; the appropriately monickered detective Will Dormer, played by Al Pacino with a minimum of his late-period bluster, is being investigated by Internal Affairs, and his partner has revealed that he intends to cooperate, and there are subtle suggestions that the shooting may not be accidental. Robin Williams plays the murderer with an effective creepiness that reminds us that when he isn't trying to be lachrymosely heartwarming, he can turn in the kind of performance that won him an Emmy nomination for his portrayal of a bereaved husband in an episode of *Homicide;* Martin Donovan's performance as the detective's partner is both subtle and robust; Hilary Swank brings a touching freshness to the rookie detective who hero-worships Dormer; and Pacino nicely conveys Dormer's increasingly weary confusion. His pouch-eyed face, as rumpled as an unmade bed, shows spiritual as well as physical weariness; he's unsurprised when the murderer reveals that he's tape-recorded an incriminating conversation, and allows Swank's eager rookie to uncover his guilt. But while the enigmatic detective in Erik Skjoldjærg's original version may be every bit as corrupt as the murderer with whom he conspires to frame an innocent man, Will Dormer is painted in broader strokes as a fundamentally decent guy who makes it clear that he despises the villain.

In Skjoldjærg's *Insomnia,* the detective sinks deeper into a mire of his own making; in Nolan's, the detective is trying to find a way out. And although Nolan's version, made with considerable style and pace, is no run-of-the-mill remake, in the final scenes Hollywood schmaltz and girl-in-peril clichés intrude. Erik Skjoldjærg's original is set in the far north of Norway, shot in clinical greys and blues, enlivened by patches of luminous white, that reflect the bleak demeanor of its Swedish detective who, played with quiet authority by Stella Skarsgård (*Breaking the Waves*), is seething with insecurity beneath his chilly efficiency. After he accidentally shoots his partner with a gun he shouldn't be carrying (unlike Swedish police, Norwegian police aren't routinely armed), guilt and the disorientation caused by his insomnia conspire towards a complete breakdown. Encounters with two different women show that he's a lot closer to the killer than he cares to admit, possessed by violent impulses that are barely restrained by an increasingly fragile veneer of self-control. It's an original and effective variation on the cliché that successful cops have far too much in common with the criminals they're employed to catch, and Skarsgård's restrained performance is every bit as effective as the grandstanding depictions of cops-gone-to-the-bad turned in by Denzel Washington in *Training Day* or Richard Gere in *Internal Affairs.* While the remake of *Insomnia* allows its detective an honourable escape and provides the hermetic closure necessary to all commercial fiction, the Norwegian original refuses to point up an easy moral; at the end, Skarsgård's detective gets neither redemption nor rest, and the last thing we see is his haunted unsleeping stare, challenging the audience through the credit crawl.

The remake of *Insomnia* was reviewed from a Warners' Region 1 disc loaded with extras. There's a commentary by Christopher Nolan that, by reordering scenes in order of shooting, provides a novel perspective on the making of the movie; an additional intermittent commentary by Hillary Swank, Wally Pfister, screenwriter Hillary Seitz, the production designer, and the editor; a single scene cut from the finished movie; two brief "Making Of" featurettes, and a third that tells us something about the hell of actual insomnia; a conversation between Nolan and Pacino; and a stills gallery, brief cast/crew biographies, and DVD-ROM features. The only extra on the Region 2 disc of the original version of *Insomnia,* released by Arrow Film Distribution, is the theatrical trailer, but if you want to buy only one version, the extras-free but thought-provoking original is the one to get.

Paul McAuley

Modesty Blaise, The Movie: Traducing Peter O'Donnell?

With the Bond movies, arguably as much influenced by the long-running newspaper strip as the Fleming novels, breaking box-office records and the *Batman* TV series establishing camp as the tone for all comic book adaptations, the late 1960s saw a run of superhero/superspy/supermodel pictures that now seem like the templates for Austin Powers. Like *Barbarella, Diabolik, Casino Royale* and the Flint or Matt Helm movies, the 1966 *Modesty Blaise* is a big international adventure with more emphasis on comic character bits and pop art design than fidelity to the original material (Peter O'Donnell's strip) or serious action-adventure. Monica Vitti, always a wonderful presence, is fundamentally miscast – she occasionally appears in the comic character's distinctive Emma Peel-look catsuit (there's a joke about getting in and out of something that doesn't appear to have a zip) and black beehive, but she mostly goes blonde and opts for summery dresses. Having made serious, ambitious genre pictures from *The Damned* (whose Elizabeth Frink statues recur here) to *The Criminal,* exiled American director Joseph Losey lightened up and freaks out (a tendency which would disastrously lead to *Boom*) and skips through a silly plot about a shipment of jewels from the British Government to an eccentric oil sheik, obviously more interested in amazing decor and costumes. Vitti might be a well-dressed blank, but there's a defining performance from Dirk Bogarde as the louche, sensitive sociopath master-crook Gabriel, sipping a drink in which a goldfish swims, staked out in the desert pleading for champagne, resisting the nagging of his penny-pinching Scots accountant (Clive Revill) and the excesses of his torture-happy sidekick Mrs Fothergill (Rosella Falk). Terence Stamp is also fun as Modesty's platonic partner Willie Garvin, joining her in a musical number that would be out of place if there were anything at all in place in the movie, and Harry Andrews and Michael Craig huff effectively as Establishment types. It's not to every taste, and the final assault on a Mediterranean island refuge by camel-riding Arab hordes perhaps does shade into *Casino Royale* anything-including-the-kitchen-sink territory, but there are a lot of lovely little things: the odd berets that unfold into gas-masks, Joe Melia as a mime silently pleading for his life under torture, tea served off a wobbling tray on Tina Aumont's breasts, gun-pointing poses off paperback covers or out of

Godard, Bogarde's wearily sighed asides and the coolest glasses ever, the guard innocently playing shoot 'em up before being transfixed by an arrow. It's all about style, but at least it genuinely has it, delivering dandyism and zero-degree cool rather than the slight plod that the Bond films always suffer through using safe-pair-of-hands directors rather than authentic crazies. The DVD is no-frills, but at least delivers anamorphic widescreen and gorgeous colour. And, be honest, wouldn't you rather watch this again than any 007 not starring Sean Connery?

Mildred Pierce

Michael Curtiz, director/Warner Home Video

When Monte Beragon (Zachary Scott), a playboy whose worthlessness is immediately apparent from his thin moustache and quivering chin, is shot dead in a shadowy beach house – a triumphantly noirish opening sequence – restaurateur Mildred Pierce (Joan Crawford) confesses to the crime and her complicated life story unfolds in a series of flashbacks. As in the other great James M Cain adaptation of the 1940s, *Double Indemnity*, a confessional narration 'explains' to us the route which has taken the central character from a brightly-lit, drably ordinary daytime world into a nightmare of carnality, criminality, corruption and chaos. Mildred walks out on her marriage to dull, struggling middle-class broker Bert (Bruce Bennett) so that she could provide for her spoiled, petulant, demanding daughter Veda (Ann Blyth). Becoming a waitress, which causes the nasty teenager to turn snobbishly against her, Mildred struggles for a living, and finally opens a restaurant, Mildred's, which becomes a successful chain. Meanwhile, she is torn between the romantic advances of the puzzled and decent Bert, the smarmily lecherous Wally (Jack Carson) and the slickly empty Monte. She marries the playboy, and he squanders her hard-won fortune while making a play for the tramp Veda. Unlike *Double Indemnity*, which is notable for Walter Neff's unflinchingly honest confession, the film leads up to a series of revelations which cast doubt over what we have been told. Made in 1945, *Mildred Pierce* is an unusual film noir, in that the amour fou which drags the central character down into the gutter inhabited by such doomed protagonists as Edward G Robinson in *Scarlet Street* or Robert Mitchum in *Out of the Past* is not sexual. Crawford's Mildred, one of the few obsessional female protagonists in the genre, is in the line of maternal sacrifice that extends throughout the women's weepie genre from *Stella Dallas* to *Terms of Endearment*, while Blyth's girlish monster (at once a snob and a slut) is a less substantial femme fatale than is usual in noir, almost like the petulant teenager who will grow up into Barbara Stanwyck's Phyllis Dietrichson, and all the more horrifying for her lack of psychotic class. The film is rooted in the shadowy alleyways of film noir, and director Michael Curtiz and cinematographer Ernest Haller use the darkest possible compositions, while composer Max Steiner overlays a driving, downbeat, relentless score to add to the oppression. A perfectly-assembled Warner Brothers' contract stable supporting cast – including Eve Arden as the heroine's traditional wisecracking girlfriend – are exactly right as a collection of variously feckless, selfish, flawed and feebler-than-Joan Crawford characters. This is a film full of night and rain, of trapped characters struggling against their situations, dragged down by their weaknesses. But *Mildred Pierce* is at least as much a woman's picture as it is a film noir; indeed, the murder investigation framework was added by screenwriter Ranald MacDougall to frame Cain's novel, which is more like soap noir than crime. The versatile and visionary Curtiz, whose only pure noir was *The Unsuspected*, was here channelled by ex-journalist producer Jerry Wald, whose allegiance to the form resulted in such female-centered psychodramas as *Humoresque*, *Caged*, *Miss Sadie Thompson* and *Peyton Place*. Wald's women suffer, but generally come through in the end, and Mildred is saved despite herself. Whereas the male protagonists of *Scarlet Street* or *Double Indemnity* were too corrupt in their love to be free even after they have murdered their scheming mistresses, Mildred can be redeemed because her maternal love, though misguided, is untainted by sin (given the posthumous image of Crawford presented by *Mommie Dearest*, this aspect of the film has a heavy irony now). Her essential strength of character, the quality which makes her movie heroine material and the quintessential Joan Crawford role, is rewarded in the understated but emotive fade-out. Warner's DVD is all you could wish – mostly thanks to a shimmering transfer that preserves the gorgeous black-and-silver look and brings out every tremor of Crawford's vocal work-out. Besides a feature-length Turner Classics documentary, *Joan Crawford: The Ultimate Movie Star*, the most significant bonus is an assembly of trailers for Crawford's Warners work – with the early *The Woman* and the late *What Ever Happened to Baby Jane?* – all-star or co-star pictures treated separately: one screen offers the full run of Crawford's Warners vehicles (*Mildred Pierce*, *Humoresque*, *Possessed*, *Flamingo Road*, *The Damned Don't Cry*, *Goodbye, My Fancy*, *This Woman is Dangerous*), showing the rise and fall of a star at a studio in perfect miniature as the co-stars get feebler (three movies with David Brian!), the parts more unsuitable or obvious reruns of Mildred, the budgets decline and the star's set jaw becomes more harridan-like.

Fingers

James Toback, director/Warner Home Video

Though he has been making odd, charged little movies – recently *Black and White* and *Harvard Man* – since the 1970s, director-writer James Toback has never really had a commercial breakthrough. His biggest credit, the script for *Bugsy*, was developed as a project for him to direct and then turned over by star Warren Beatty to the more biddable Barry Levinson. He may well be one of those figures whose entire career consists of a footnote to one brilliant debut feature. And *Fingers*, from 1978, remains an impressive, exciting and strange film, related to but intriguingly different from the New York crime/culture hybrids fashioned with the same star (Harvey Keitel) by Martin Scorsese (*Mean Streets*) and Abel Ferrara (*Bad Lieutenant*). Jimmy Angelelli (Keitel) is an almost absurdly complex character, who would risk being ridiculous if Keitel didn't bring such intense conviction to the part. With a croaking hood father (Michael V Gazzo) who needs him to work as a strong-arm collector for his small-time loan shark operation and an elegant but institutionalised mother (Marian Seldes) whose career as a concert pianist he would like to follow, Jimmy walks the streets with his pre-walkman portable cassette player, providing his own doo-wop soundtrack, his fingers relentlessly drumming out the moves for the Bach piece he wants to play at his Carnegie Hall audition. Over the course of the film, Jimmy gets back into gangsterdom, becomes obsessed with a sculptress/hooker (Tisa Farrow), flunks his audition (thrown off by a night in jail and, unnervingly, getting trapped briefly in the lift on his way up to the rehearsal room), has his own sexuality repeatedly challenged (few actors can convey not enjoying sex as well as Keitel does – he is exactly as pained when fucking Tanya Roberts in a changing room to intimidate her defaulting debtor boyfriend as he is receiving what Toback is proud to call the most accurate prostate exam in the cinema), and winds up avenging his father with a scrappy, convincing stairwell murder (the victim is Tony Sirico, now Paulie Walnuts on *The Sopranos*). It's a film of brilliant, disturbing, elliptical scenes and shocking moments – player Dreems (Jim Brown) banging two hookers' heads together – with a real sense of a life in danger. It could be the origin story of any villain, with the bloodied, naked, animal Keitel of the final scene – all aspirations to love and culture gone – the just-born sociopath who will become the monstrous gangsters who crop up in so many films and TV shows. Warner's DVD presents a nice letterboxed widescreen print – there's a bit of grain and a lot of rough edge, but that's how the film is supposed to look. Aside from a tiny chat on independent film with Toback and Keitel, the extra of note is a commentary from the writer-director that provides background anecdotes about the cast and crew and the production, indicating how much of Jim Brown's role comes from his own life, but is also unusually willing to explore thematic and character depths that many filmmakers shy away from in these tracks for fear of sounding pretentious.

Kim Newman

NATASHA COOPER: WRITING CRIME

*CT prides itself on the number of top crime writers who are happy to write for these pages – and here's **Natasha Cooper** (aka Clare Layton), regularly to be found as reviewee at the back of CT for her Trish Maguire crime treats, talking about the crime writer's life…*

Writing a novel is a most peculiar business. It requires a dizzying mixture of self-absorption and self-abnegation. If the novel isn't 'yours' it won't work; but if you insist on your own way when your editor says 'this bit stinks', you're likely to end up unread and on the scrap heap. There has to be something of you in all your characters to make them live, but then you have to rub yourself out while you listen to their voices in your head and make them move realistically around your plot. They can't put your world right for you; they have to be free to fulfil their own destinies, even though it is you who have invented their fate. It's no wonder that writers are prey to delusion, paranoia, drink, and depression. In fact, the only surprise is that so many survive to see their books through to publication. Then comes the worst bit. When you've written the thing and been through the whole tough process of editing and rewriting, you can't rest. You have to set out on the same journey all over again for the next maelstrom of violence you plan to whip up for your readers' delectation.

The first days – or weeks – of any novel are painful. Words either withhold themselves completely, or gush out in such a torrent you know they won't tell your reader anything useful. You try on this story, then that; you see landscapes and shapes within them that draw you on, only to discover you've been following a will o'the wisp into a morass of meaningless verbiage. And then one day, without your really noticing, the words smooth themselves out into a regular pace. You know where you're going with them, and at last the ground beneath you feels firm. You find that you care about the strange new people your imagination has wished on you, and you see new possibilities in your familiar players. It's not all easy from then on, of course. You can always fall into fatal over-confidence and come to grief. Writing fiction is like riding a bicycle. Unless you keep braced and pedalling, you will fall off. Speed is exciting but dangerous.

I have been writing fiction full-time since 1986, 17 years of deadlines and characters, metaphors and grammar, invention and correction. I love it. In spite of all the frustrations and anxieties, I can't think of anything I would rather do. And yet I feel as though I've hardly started. There is so much to learn. Every novel completed teaches me more about the craft of writing and about psychology, my own as much as my characters'. When I started, it never occurred to me to consider writing a crime novel. I began with historical romance. And yet, looking back now, I see that even then I was much more interested in violence than in love. In those days it was the cruelty of war that grabbed my attention, rather than that of one individual to another. My first novel was set in the First Afghan War and my heroine, gentle and frightened though she was, stabbed a man to death amid positive fountains of blood. I went on to the Russian Revolution, the Second World War, the Suez Crisis, and, in my last historical, Paris in 1968. At that point I had to stop. I remember 1968 far too clearly to be happy with the idea of it as 'history'. And so I turned to crime, where the violence is on a much smaller scale and yet one so horribly intimate that it has even more influence on the people who endure and perpetrate it. And even on the witnesses and investigators.

My latest crime novel, *A Place of Safety*, brings both kinds of violence together. Most of it takes place in London at the beginning of the 21st century, but there are also scenes set in a frontline casualty clearing station in France during the First World War. As I began to think about the novel, well over two years ago, I realised that just as every human being is affected by the experiences of his parents and grandparents, so all crimes have their ancestry, too. There are none that have no causes in what went before. My intention with the novel, apart from whisking readers into worlds I hoped would interest and excite them, was to explore the roots of both character and violence. The research took me to places I had never expected. I started by reading First World War memoirs, both of the fighting men and the women who nursed them when they were wounded, memoirs my character Trish Maguire would also read within the novel. Like her, I spent time in the Imperial War Museum, standing in the recreated First World War trench, hearing the guns and letting my imagination feed me with the terror the real inhabitants must have felt. Their courage and endurance awed me. In lighter moments, I attended fine art auctions, walked round some of the innumerable small galleries that exist in London, all the time dreaming up a fictional one and the people who would work in it and carry my story to its conclusion. But there were other – emotional – journeys I had to take, too. Working on *A Place of Safety* took me into the minds of people teetering on the narrow boundary between terror and aggression. It taught me more about duplicity and exploitation than I really wanted to know. And it ended with a reassurance I had no idea I needed. All in all, it was quite an adventure.

For me, it's over now. I am plunging into quite different worlds as I begin my journey into the new book, and put *A Place of Safety* into the hands of the most important person in the whole writing business – you, the reader.

***A Place of Safety* will be published in hardback in the UK by Simon & Schuster in July and then by St Martin's Press in the USA**

Natasha Cooper

CAMPBELL'S CRIMES

Mark Campbell

CT is always grateful for Mark Campbell's insights, even if we don't always agree with them. His titles for the Pocket Essentials series include Sherlock Holmes, Agatha Christie *and* Carry On Films *(we don't hold the latter against him)...*

First, an apology. To those of you who waited on tenterhooks (just what *is* a tenterhook¿) for the second instalment of this fledgling column, its disappearance from the last issue of *Crime Time* can only have been a bitter disappointment to you. For you see, just when I was getting up to speed on my chequered writing career, along comes a veritable boatful of worthier articles, interviews, reviews and, ahem, adverts. Poor old Barry Forshaw (or, as us contributors like to call him, 'Barry') spent many a sleeping night before finally picking up the phone and calling me in person to inform me of the sad news: "No column this time," he said, fighting back those tears in a way that only hardened journo-type editors can. "Oh that's all right," I replied gamely, one ear full of shampoo suds. "I didn't know what to write anyway." Now, 'not knowing what to write anyway' is a bad thing for a writer. Actually, let me put it more strongly – it is a very bad thing. The difference between knowing what to write and not knowing what to write is the difference between being a writer (2% of the population) and thinking you're a writer (98%). From my time spent working at the ever more free-thinking Books Etc, I can vouchsafe that pretty much everyone had either written a book, was working on a book, or was thinking about working on a book. Or a screenplay. Or a collection of poetry. Of those people, none – to my knowledge – have ever had anything professionally published. No, wait, tell a lie, there is one. My one-time sitcom co-writer (I'll save that story for another column) has had his fair share of success – and if the world was a less cruel place he'd be having far more of it. Success, that is. Oh yes, and a bookseller I didn't know from another branch won a two-book deal with HarperCollins while a former Boxtree rep I knew vaguely had a first novel published with Hodder (I think). Good luck to both of them, but it's a poor hit rate for the many years I spent in the company of all those frustrated writers.

So, not knowing what to write is certainly a handicap for any writer. But then again, even if you know exactly what to write and which market to aim it at, you've still got to go and write the bloody thing. Alfred Hitchcock once told an interviewer – probably François Truffaut – how bored he was by the filming process. As far as he was concerned, the script and storyboard were the main things. To actually have to get a camera out and film the scenes was a chore to be endured rather than enjoyed. That's the way a lot of writers think, myself included. The idea for an article might be fully formed in my mind. But the process of forcing it out of my headspace and having to wrestle it down, struggling, against its will, onto a computer screen is a uniquely writerly kind of torture. But at least there's something there to begin with. Many writers I've spoken to have likened the writing process to giving birth. The analogy is a good one (although real childbirth is easier), but at least you know you're giving birth to something that is actually there. Far worse is a phantom pregnancy, in which you sit down at a blank screen, full of expectation and hope, and wait. And wait. And wait. For what? For the creative muse? For the perfect sentence? For the next instalment of *Diagnosis Murder*? Not knowing what to write can happen to the best of us. In point of fact, it's usually 'real' writers who suffer from this problem. Wannabe writers have it easy – they always know *what* to write, they just don't get off their arses and do it. Professional writers quickly discover that ideas are not unlimited. Churning out articles and reviews and opinion pieces does not automatically mean you will continue churning out articles, reviews and opinion pieces. There comes a point when the most prolific scribe will suddenly say, "That's it – my brain has officially turned to toxic sludge. I don't possess a single decent new thought. I am entirely washed out of creativity, imagination and insight." Either that, or they'll just scream. Then they'll either a) walk the dog, b) go to the pub, or c) keep on writing. Yes, it is possible to write 'through' writer's block, provided you don't mind going back the next day and picking up the pieces. Many fine novels have gone through extensive redrafting from their ludicrously improbable first drafts. Rewriting is so much easier than writing.

Of course the worst sort of writing project to cope with when you've run out of ideas is the column. I would say 'regular column', but thus far this description does not apply to Campbell's Crimes. Irregular column, let's say. I mean, I would definitely have come up with something for the last issue, but at the point of sitting down and writing something, my mind was not exactly blossoming with ideas. For the record, the last issue of *Crime Time* dealt with that thorny problem of violence in crime fiction (they'd dealt with sex a while back), and I was fine-tuning my grey cells when Barry's call came through. So – what would I have said? Well, I could summarise my unwritten column in one word: 'context'. Violence is everywhere, all around us, in our daily lives and on the news and on the big screen. Physical, mental or verbal violence – it's everywhere we look. And what makes it work, and what makes it not, is that little word called 'context'. If you were walking to the newsagent and a man came up and hit you on the back of the head with a hammer, you'd be rather peeved. But if you'd tried to hold up a hardware store with a flick-knife after being sacked from your job and losing your wife and children, and the proprietor's assistant came up behind you with the aforesaid weapon, it wouldn't be quite so much of a surprise when your brains shot out of your ears. *Reservoir Dogs* is supposed to be violent. It's not. *Se7en,* laughably, is supposed to be violent. It's not. But if I happen to turn the TV on to a Saturday afternoon Western, I'm amazed at the violent behaviour on display. Cowboys and Indians (mostly Indians) are mown down all over the shop. They fall off horses, down hills and from the roofs of saloon bars. They groan, tumble and lurch dramatically to the ground. All very impressive. All very violent. Why don't we criticise scenes like these? Why pick on a handful of high-profile feature films or TV series to demonise? Perhaps it's because we look on the Western, rather oddly, as a form of entertainment. A contemporary story with as much shooting and killing as a Western would be condemned as too violent. Which is why a film that shows no explicit violence at all *(Se7en)* is criticised, usually by those who haven't seen it, as being too violent. Sure, there's implied violence, there's the aftermath of violence, but as for deaths per minute, it's way down the bottom of the list. Anything historical is allowed to, literally, get away with murder. That goes for anything fantastical too. *From Dusk Till Dawn* becomes a total bloodbath, but because the antagonists aren't human (sorry, spoiled the plot), we aren't supposed to be worried. Forget the fact that a 'realistic' film is as much a construct as a horror film – different rules seem to apply for different genres. The crime genre, certainly as far as the written word goes, is not especially violent. Most of the books I review for this publication are not wildly explicit for the sake of it. Where there's a murder, there's usually a salient reason for its inclusion. And the murder doesn't have to be described in much detail; the journey of hammer through skull can be tossed off in a few words. Or a few pages if your name's Brett Easton Ellis. Agatha Christie wrote virtually bloodless mysteries, yet hers are some of the most violent in the genre.

We've discussed (or rather, I've discussed, you're just listening) physical violence. But let's not forget the other sort – psychological violence. Threats, intimidation, coercion, bullying in any shape or form – these are no less disturbing for the characters or the readers. Psychological warfare is the bedrock upon which any good drama is set, from *Who Killed Virginia Woolf* to *The Birthday Party.* You don't have to shoot someone or drive a hammer through their cranium, you can be far more imaginative than that. Good psychological crime fiction abounds, from Barbara Vine to Tony Strong. For the funniest and most disturbing use of this unique brand of violence, try Magnus Mills' masterpiece *All Quiet on the Orient Express.* Think *Last of the Summer Wine* written by the Marquis de Sade and you'll get the idea.

And let's not forget about the consequences of these actions. Violence plays its part in the telling of a story, but you also need to know what happens afterwards – the consequences of a violent act are more wide-reaching than the act itself. Any crime hero worth his salt will suffer the occasional twinge at the suffering he causes to others. This separates bad writing from good; good from great. Of course, with some heroes those twinges take on operatic proportions – Ian Rankin's Edinburgh detective John Rebus went through a virtual breakdown caused by work-related stress and a particularly galling personal tragedy (poor sod – what's he done to anybody?). With others, a black look and a few mumbled regrets are all that passes for guilt. Either way, the impact of violence on the main players should not go undescribed. In a nutshell, instead of talking about 'sex and violence', why not talk about 'context and violence'? And speaking of which, as you're asking, one of the most violent crime books I've ever read is *A Simple Plan* by Scott Smith. It's a compelling thriller in which the escalating scenes of mayhem arise organically from the twists of the plot and the motivation of the central character. If you've seen the film, you've only seen half of it – read the book to find out how bad it really gets. And now, having beaten the record set by the late Mary Whitehouse for the most mentions of the word 'violence' in a single article, I'll sign off. You'll be here next issue – but will I?

Mark Campbell

THE MAMMOTH BOOK OF
FUTURE COPS
CONTRIBUTIONS FROM MICHAEL MARSHALL-SMITH, PHILIP K. DICK, J. D. ROBB, IAIN M. BANKS, KIM NEWMAN, PAT CADIGAN, JON COURTNEY-GRIMWOOD, KURT VONNEGUT, AND MANY MORE . . .
Dark tales from a future where science and society may be twisted but the human connection still remains
EDITED BY MAXIM JAKUBOWSKI

TO THE MAX: MAXIM JAKUBOWSKI

His own books have earned him the sobriquet King of the Erotic Thriller; he's one of the genre's premier editors... Mr ***Maxim Jakubowski****.*

Clea's Moon by Edward Wright (Orion, £10.99)

An interesting first novel by a new American author discovered by the Crime Writers' Association Debut Dagger competition, *Clea's Moon* serves up a highly original protagonist and mixed-up hero and background, but is let down by a lack of pace. John Ray Horn was once B-movie cowboy hero Sierra Lane, until the fateful day he assaulted his producer's son and ended up in jail and boycotted by 1940s Hollywood. Now, he makes ends meet by collecting debts for his ex-Indian sidekick Joseph Mad Crow. The visit of an old friend in need of help plunges him into the vortex of Los Angeles' post WW2 underworld and the shady associations of old and new money. The quest becomes highly personal after his friend's suspicious

death and the discovery of pornographic photos of paedophiliacs at large, involving his own step-daughter. Both a quest for redemption and a clever variation on *Chinatown* and how LA was built, Wright's tale has sterling ingredients but unfolds at too leisurely a rhythm. More urgency next time?

***Spiral* by Joseph Geary (Simon & Schuster, £12.99)**

Advertised by its publisher as 'Jackson Pollock meets *The Silence of the Lambs*', this is more a case of Francis Bacon meets *The Collector*, which in my eyes puts it into another league altogether. A deeply flawed writer and biographer is about to publish his definitive biography of shady 1960s cult artist Frank Spira when new information comes to light. As Greer becomes increasingly obsessed by what becomes a murder case, he is inexorably drawn into a web of infamy, secrets and sheer horror which puts his whole work into question. His pursuit of the truth destroys his marriage as he moves from New York galleries and museums to Tangiers in a quest for revelation. The twists and turns of the thriller are exemplary and the gradual unveiling of the truth behind Spira's lost paintings flirts with abominable new degrees of dread. In addition, the book offers a witty dissection of the contemporary art world, monomaniac collectors and a chilling study of obsession. This is the stuff of nightmares and one to savour slowly.

***The Frost Fair* by Edward Marston (Allison & Busby, £17.99)**

Marston, a pen name for a highly prolific British crime writer and ex-*Z Cars* scriptwriter, is one of the field's hidden treasures, a craftsman who for years has launched countless historical mystery series which public libraries never seem to be able to keep on their shelves long enough, even though his books move from publisher to publisher. Consummate storytelling, a love of period and astute characterisation and plotting are the marks of all his books, and this fourth in a series featuring architect Christopher Redmayne and Puritan constable Jonathan Bale, set in Restoration London after the Great Fire of 1666, is no exception. The Thames has frozen over during one of the coldest winters for years and a frost fair is held on the thick ice. When a child gets into trouble on a thinner patch of ice, a grizzly discovery is made and the body of an Italian fencing master is discovered, only for Redmayne's brother to soon be accused of the murder. The exoticism of the past comes to life with brilliant colours, combined with a perfect whodunit. Who needs more?

When the Women Come Out to Dance
by Elmore Leonard (Viking, £15.99)

The economical prose of Elmore Leonard is particularly well suited for the short story form, and it is surprising that in a career spanning four decades he has so seldom worked in the genre. This is his first collection in the crime field (although it has a story in common with his Western collection *The Tonto Woman*). As ever with the hardboiled sage of Detroit, there are no big themes or complicated plots, just exquisite characterisation brought to life by the sparest of prose and dialogue. From vignettes to novellas, some of which bring back familiar characters from past novels in tales that could well have initially been rough sketches for books past or to come, we have a procession of female characters with both balls to spare and a profane way with words, each righting wrongs in devious ways against a panorama of wonderful grotesques: errant Pakistani plastic

surgeons with dreams of murder, stuntmen in search of revenge, white supremacist domestic bullies, garrulous baseball players, neo-Nazi miners. Leonard here is a master at play in the fields of human nature, make no mistake about it.

Maxim Jakubowski

Maxim Jakubowski's latest book is The Mammoth Book of Future Cops *(Robinson £6.99)*

DAVID AND THE SEVERAL GOLIATHS

Russell James

Russell James, ex-chairman of the Crime Writers' Association and almost the only crime writer to have no detectives in his books, continues his mission to discover what makes writers tick.

Back in CT31 I fulminated against the way that profit-averse publishers – supposedly run by sober-minded accountants – stake all their money on a few sleek horses from their stable, printing huge numbers and then bribing all and sundry to lash out on the things. Ah, that was then, so last season. Publishers' latest ruse for throwing money away – one that so appalled the *Bookseller* magazine that one of its editorials ran wet with tears from the editor's eye – has been to take the most certain profit-generators (that's best-sellers to you and me) and to slash the price so deeply that the profit disappears. Perhaps the rot began last year with the celebrated case of *Harry Potter and the Goblet of Fire*, a book which hundreds of thousands of children of all ages had been desperate for all year: it was the must-have book for Christmas. Must-have merchandise is not price-sensitive because we must have it. But publishers, it seems, thought they must get rid of it. At any price. It made no difference that this particular publisher was Bloomsbury, one that without the unexpected windfall of *Potter* would by now have crumbled into oblivion, one that prior to Potter's arrival was known mainly for the speed with which its titles were remaindered (they had hardbacks into remainder shops before the paperback came out), one that now rides high in the profitability top ten and prides itself that its astonishing revival is due to its financial acumen rather than to its fairy godmother J K Rowling. Bloomsbury was no more financially acute than is this week's winner of the National Lottery. But although Bloomsbury is only one of Britain's self-immolating publishers, let's stick with them to see just how insane (my euphemism for inept) the publishing industry has become. That last *Harry Potter* was priced at £14.99 – but how few of us paid the full price. We would have done, of course, it was a must-have item – many customers would have paid more – but we didn't have to. Normal discounting (another euphemism, this time for disregard of profits) might have seen *Potter* on sale at perhaps £16.99, allowably discounted down to £14.99. But no. So eager was Bloomsbury to throw money away, so staggeringly generous were the bulk discounts, that mass market retailers were able to reduce this must-have-at-any-price treasure from £14.99 to as low as £8.99. Non mass market retailers (a euphemism for friendly local bookshops) couldn't even *buy* it from their wholesalers at £8.99, let alone sell it at a competitive price. Some declined to compete.

Faced with the inevitable – that customers would pop into a supermarket and buy it there – many small bookshops stocked no copies at all. They'd order it for you, were you determined to be extravagant, but they expected you to buy the book elsewhere. (Some booksellers bought a copy or two from the supermarket and sold you that. At a profit.) I cannot blame them for giving up the fight. My own tactic, had I run a friendly local bookshop, would have been to hunt down the cheapest local outlet, to buy the book from them and then sell at an even lower price. A huge sign would have blazed in my window: *Harry Potter. This Week Only. £7.99 – cheaper than anywhere in town* – adding in smaller font: *when you spend £15 on any other books*. I'd win three ways: first, my £1 loss on *Potter* would be offset by the profit on the £15; second, my offer would appeal to book buyers, as opposed to mere gift buyers; third, it would be a splendid one-in-the-eye for big multiples. Just as I was about to propose this wheeze to any independent bookseller who would listen, along came a host of kamikaze publishers to shoot themselves in the other foot. Not content with throwing most of their profit away in unsustainably high discounts, they now proceeded to practically give away the rest of their stock. No, correction: to give away only their most popular, best-selling stock.

(You know, the stuff that makes money.) How did they do this? Well, at the very time publishers were bribing retail chains to reduce their over-printed book runs, they struck deals with Book Club Associates and The Book People to buy top titles at a ludicrous 75% discount (selling to these sharks at barely more than cost), allowing them to sell prime stock even cheaper than supermarkets and to cut authors' royalties to almost nil.

A brief history: years ago, when publishers were run by folk who genuinely loved books, the lovingly crafted creations were issued first in hardback, then a year later in cheaper paperback. At this one-year point, when the cream of sales had passed, book club editions were permitted to emerge alongside the paperbacks. These editions were usually printed by book clubs themselves, on inferior stock, and did little damage to the publishers' sales – and they paid authors a much reduced royalty. A few book clubs were allowed to bring out more upmarket 'simultaneous publications', marked with the book club logo rather than the publishers', and they sold these at 25% below original price. So far, fairly good. Then the one-year rule was squashed to six months. OK, we live in a faster world. But then... Publishers, seduced (my euphemism for hoodwinked) by book clubs' guiles, and greedy for massive volume sales (who cares about profit or the authors' royalties?) dumped vast quantities on the willing book clubs at knockdown prices and with no restrictions on holding back from 'simultaneous publication'. Result? Today, brand new titles are offered to the bemused public at £18.99 (say) from their local bookshop, £12.99 from supermarkets, and £6.99 (or less) from BCA or TBP. And the TBP edition doesn't even carry a different logo! It's identical to the publisher's own, newly released edition. Can you imagine any other manufacturer following such a suicidal policy? Buy my latest product from the regular dealer at full price, or (shades of Petticoat Lane), "Tell you what, ma'am, I'll cut me profit to the bone and let you have it at half price from these – er – general wotsit dealers" or, incredibly, "I'll dump the lot on these pile 'em high merchants – from day one – and let you have 'em at a price way below what my regular dealers have to pay wholesale."

In all of these cut-price deals, the poor author is disembowelled. Royalty per book is cut from (say) £1.40 to 10p. Hopefully, a lot more people will read the book – but if gaining an audience was the author's only objective he could have posted the text on the internet and let people read it there for free. But that isn't the author's objective; the poor sod is struggling to live. He hasn't been involved in the high-level financial shenanigans; he's an outsider, like you and me. No, correction again: he isn't an outsider – he's paying for the shenanigans with a direct loss of income. But given that publishers have reduced themselves to the level of gibbering idiots, how can an author fight back? I wish I knew. To me, there are only two ways out of this. Either, as I hope, the current practice of chucking designer merchandise straight out to the street market will quickly demonstrate itself to be insane, and publishers will begin the uphill slog of both reigning back massive discounts and re-educating the public to pay a realistic price; or we writers will have to stand up for our rights. (Literally: because an author owns the rights.) But don't look to authors of *my* lowly status to make the stand. Frankly my dear, the major publishers don't give a damn what I write or say. But how happy are the world's top authors to see their royalties drain away? How happy are their agents? When will one stand up to the publishers and say no, tear up your contract – here are my terms: my royalty is 10% (or 7.5%, whatever) of *the full retail price*. If you want to sell stock to cut-throat dealers, that's your affair – but my royalty will not suffer. Not by one penny. Bear in mind that for a publisher to pay a hardback royalty between (say) £1.40 to £1.90 would eliminate his measly profit on a book offloaded for £3.50 to bulk traders, and you can see the inevitable result. No publisher would refuse to sign their top-selling authors. Such authors call the tune. Such authors can stop their titles being flogged off to this wretched new breed of pile 'em high barrow boys. If they – or their agents – would band together to force through a new, more equitable, standard contract, then – and only then – might there be a ray of hope for the rest of us.

So, Mr Grisham and Mr Rankin; so, Ms Cornwell and Martina Cole – how about carrying the flag for us? At a time like this, we need a hero.

Russell's latest book in Britain is Pick Any Title *(The Do Not Press) and in America is* The Annex *(Five Star Mysteries)*

CRIME ON TV: A TALE OF TWO HALVES

Charles Waring

For a show that was flatly rejected by two major US TV networks when it was first proposed by creator Dick Wolf as a potential new prime-time crime drama at the tail-end of the 1980s, NBC's *Law & Order* has not only demonstrated remarkable durability but has also exerted considerable influence on other TV cop programmes. The critically acclaimed show even managed to stave off the threat of cancellation in its third season. Apparently, NBC TV executives consulted their demographic data and discovered that very few women watched the series. Believing that *Law & Order* was much too male-dominated in regard to its cast and characters, the show earned a reprieve from the executioner's axe by the hasty addition of prominent female characters, which apparently managed to entice a good portion of distaff viewers to tune in to the show. *Law & Order* is the brainchild of Madison Avenue advertising exec-turned-TV mogul and producer, Dick Wolf (who, significantly, had worked behind the scenes on the pioneering cop shows, *Hill Street Blues* and *Miami Vice* in the 1980s). Featuring a memorable theme tune by composer Mike Post (famed for his music to *Hill Street Blues* and *NYPD Blue*) *Law & Order* aired on US TV to critical acclaim way back in 1990, following on from a pilot episode that was made two years' earlier. Thirteen long years and several prestigious Emmy awards down the line, *Law & Order* is still fresh, still relevant and still in production – and it lays claim to being the longest running primetime show on US television. What's even more remarkable is that the show is more popular than it's ever been, with phenomenal US audience ratings to prove it. But what makes *Law & Order's* longevity even more surprising is the fact that it has survived a veritable plethora of personnel changes in regard to its cast. If you tuned into the show during the early 1990s when actors Michael Moriarty, Richard Brooks and George Dzundza starred, I dare say that you wouldn't recognise any of the characters that inhabit the current series. And yet despite this protean quality, *Law & Order* patently doesn't suffer from instability – its major strength is that the story takes precedence over everything. Characters are important, of course, but they do not drive the show – ultimately they are expendable. The reason for this, I think, is that *Law & Order* doesn't venture too deeply into the personal lives of its characters. Consequently, there's no distracting soap opera aspect to the show – rather, it depicts people in a work environment where personal problems are put on the back burner. For all its myriad characters, *Law & Order* has stuck almost rigidly to a simple, watertight format. Put in a nutshell, *Law & Order* is defined by three words: crime, investigation and prosecution. In the first half of the programme, the viewer sees a crime committed, which is then investigated by detectives who aim to bring the perpetrators to justice. The second half of the programme then focuses its attention on the attempted prosecution of the wrongdoers by lawyers from the DA's office. Adhering to this format and using storylines that are frequently based on topical issues (and even inspired by news headlines) has meant that the show can shed characters without losing its audience and popularity. Viewers don't switch on to follow the trajectory of a character's life, but to unravel the often complex twists and turns of a crime story as it unfolds from the street to the court.

In terms of its well-crafted storylines, *Law & Order* has covered a lot of territory – there are plenty of gruesome murders, certainly, but it has also covered such varied topics as child abuse, police corruption, euthanasia, medical malpractice, racism, gang rape, kidnapping and organised crime. It's not gritty in a visceral way like the groundbreaking HBO series *Homicide: Life on the Street* and *The Sopranos* – it is, however, deeply rooted in reality and its offers a vivid and insightful depiction of the American legal system, with all its attendant complexities. Shot on location in New York, *Law & Order* has, on average 36 speaking roles per one-hour episode. Consequently, over its 13 seasons, the series has employed the services of hundreds of Big Apple actors. In fact, it's reckoned that at least 150 Tony-nominated thespians have appeared in the show during its 13-year life. Many big names have also participated, ranging from current Hollywood big hitters like Samuel L Jackson and Julia Roberts to veteran character actors James Earl Jones, Robert Vaughn and Eli Wallach. Some actors, like William H Macy, Philip Seymour Hoffmann and Aida Turturro (best known for her role in *The Sopranos* as Tony Soprano's sister, Janice) have been in the show several times, but on each occasion appeared as different characters. More recently, *Law & Order* has become something of a TV franchise, spawning three successful spin-off series: *Criminal Intent* (which uniquely sees crime from the criminal's perspective), *Special*

Victim's Unit (a gritty show that concentrates on crimes of a sexual nature) and *Crime & Punishment*. There's even an interactive online *Law & Order* game for those devotees who can't get enough of the show.

The inaugural episode kicked off with Michael Moriarty as Executive Assistant DA Ben Stone, Richard Brooks as his sidekick, Paul Robinette, and the corpulent figure of George Dzundza as Detective Sgt Max Greevey. The DA was a character called Adam Schiff, an irascible, laconic man who could usually be found in his office chomping on a sandwich. Schiff, who was expertly played by veteran Actors' Studio method man, Steven Hill, was an ever-present character on the show until he packed his lunch box away in 2000. In the current series, Sam Waterston (who played key roles in the memorable Hollywood movies *The Great Gatsby* and *The Killing Fields*) acts the part of the hard-nosed Executive Assistant District Attorney, Jack McCoy, whilst actress Elizabeth Rohm plays the Assistant District Attorney, Serena Southerlyn. Arthur Branch, the New District Attorney (who replaced Dianne Wiest's character, Nora Lewin), is played by none other than former Republican Senator, Fred Thompson. Although he trained as a lawyer, Thompson is no novice when it comes to acting – he appeared in many Hollywood movies prior to his being elected to the US Senate in 1994. Out of the courtroom and on the street you'll find detectives Lennie Briscoe and his partner, Ed Greene. An acerbic and wily NYPD detective, Briscoe is played by the bloodhound-faced Jerry Orbach (Orbach is also one of the longest serving cast members, having done nine years). Briscoe's boss is the tough African-American precinct lieutenant, Anita Van Buren (played by S Epatha Merkeson). *Law & Order* came to Britain soon after its US premiere, when it was acquired by the BBC in 1991. However, it failed to reach a wide audience due to a late-night programming slot and, after transmitting a couple of series, the Beeb dropped it. Until the series turned up to liven up Saturday evenings on the much-maligned Channel 5 a couple of years ago, many had assumed that the show was long dead. Of course, *Law & Order* must face its own death sentence at some point in the future but so far it has endured for 13 years. Unlucky for some maybe – but definitely not for *Law & Order*. With over 250 episodes already made, it's scheduled to remain in production until 2005. And by that time, it will be the longest running police show of all time.

Sources:
www.nbc.com/Law_&_Order
www.law&ordergame.com

Charles Waring

CT MUSIC

Charles Waring

The 1960s was the decade in which the spy movie came of age. But it was British rather than American cinematic secret agents that led the way. America could only offer insubstantial cartoon-like figures in the form of Flint and Matt Helm. But we Brits had James Bond and Harry Palmer. Franchised into futurity, Bond is still going, of course. As for Harry Palmer, he may not have made an impact comparable with Bond, but he helped catapult Michael Caine to stardom and is affectionately remembered by movie buffs. It goes without saying that Bond and Palmer were poles apart regarding the two worlds they inhabited: although they both had a proclivity for 'birds' and life's luxuries, it was more like a case of the gregarious playboy and the plebeian loner. Bond, the least conspicuous of fictional espionage men, was all about glamour and high-voltage action: fast cars and even faster women. The bespectacled, raincoat-attired figure of Harry Palmer, on the other hand, seemed almost humdrum by comparison. Despite fundamental differences in character, Bond and Palmer possessed a significant common denominator when it came to their depiction on the silver screen in the early 1960s: Harry Saltzman. The legendary American movie mogul and producer was responsible for getting the first Harry Palmer film, *The Ipcress File*, off the ground in 1965 in addition to his integral role alongside Albert Broccoli in producing the James Bond films. Furthermore, John Barry, whose music graced the most of the early Bond movies, supplied the soundtrack to *The Ipcress File*. Those who had heard Barry's often virile and energetic music accompanying *From Russia With Love* and *Goldfinger* may have been surprised that the composer could be so adept at creating music for a film where atmosphere and mood prevailed over action. At long last, Barry's original score to *The Ipcress File* makes its CD debut (Silva Screen FILMCD 105), complete with snippets of dialogue from the film. The main theme (entitled *A Man Alone*), which features an obscure, metallic-sounding instrument called a cimbalom, is beautifully understated and perfect for creating the film's low-key yet slightly sinister and funereal atmosphere. According to the CD's illuminating liner notes, Barry's inspiration was Anton Karas' score to Carol Reed's 1949 movie, *The Third Man* (they also state that the cloth-eared Saltzman detested Barry's score – but then he also believed that *Goldfinger's* title-song performed by Shirley Bassey would never become a hit!). The theme to *The Ipcress File* returns in several ingenious different guises, most notably in the form of a finger clicking saxophone-led jazz piece and a slow, mournful, blues-tinged arrangement. A superlative reissue – and highly recommended.

And talking of Bond, Silva Screen Records has just issued a four-CD box set in association with the International James Bond Fan Club entitled, *The James Bond Collection* (Silva Screen TVPMCD 808). Issued to celebrate Bond's 40th anniversary, key musical moments from every 007 film (except the latest, *Die Another Day*) are performed by the redoubtable City of Prague Philharmonic Orchestra conducted by Nic Raine. Employing surround-sound technology, the performances of material from the likes of John Barry, Monty Norman and more recent Bond composers, Eric Serra and David Arnold, are colourful and dynamic. In addition to 54 individual music tracks, this attractively packaged item (which retails at the price of a single full-price CD) is enhanced by plot synopses and cast/character lists for each Bond film. Look out for official remasters and expanded versions of the original EMI Bond soundtrack albums in 2003.

Also out on Silva Screen is an entertaining musical anthology devoted to John Carpenter movie themes. Carpenter, of course, is not only a writer and film director but an accomplished musician too and has often created his own, distinctly minimalist soundtracks. *The Essential John Carpenter Film Music Collection* (FILMCD 363) features some of Carpenter's own brooding, often disquieting electronic pieces (*Dark Star*, *Assault on Precinct 13*, *Halloween*, *Escape From New York* and the haunting *The Fog*) along with music by Ennio Morricone (*The Thing*), George Thorogood (*Christine*) and Jack Nitzche (*Starman*). The music is mostly re-created by synthesiser wizard, Gareth Williams, whose arrangements stick closely to the original movie scores. Over 70 minutes of thrills, spills and spine-tingling chills that serve as an ideal introduction to a great American auteur's movie music.

Charles Waring

THE VERDICT

Blind to the Bones
Stephen Booth
HarperCollins, £17.99, 0007130651
A dark and powerful novel by a writer of great skill. It's almost May Day, and on the desolate moors of Dark Peak, the villagers of Withens are dying. One has been battered to death and left for the crows to find; another chose the wrong time to call on a neighbour. And one has been dead for two years – though not everyone will believe it. DC Ben Cooper's attempts to solve the killings come up against an impenetrable barrier in the shape of the Oxley family. Descendants of tunnel-builders, they stick to their own area like the sheep on the hillsides, passing on secret knowledge through generations and guarding their traditions from the likes of Cooper. Stephen Booth enjoys walking the hills of the Peak District, in which his crime novels are set, and the sense of place is palpable. *Blind to the Bones* is the follow-up to his psychological thrillers, *Blood on the Tongue, Dancing with the Virgins* (which was short listed for the 2001 Gold Dagger Awards), and *Black Dog.* It's an impressive body of work from an accomplished writer.

White Doves at Morning
James Lee Burke
Orion, £12.99, 0752856502

The Civil War isn't buried very deep beneath the swampy bayou soil of Dave Robicheaux's Louisiana, so it's logical James Lee Burke should write a novel set in the Civil War. And because the past is so much with his characters, it's no surprise that it features his ancestor Willie Burke, who is enough like Robicheaux to suggest some cross-fertilisation back in the past. This historical novel's strengths are very much those of the Robicheaux series. Burke is a sensitive man, who goes to fight for a cause in which he can't believe, because he won't be thought a coward. What he sees in combat effects him just as Dave's experiences in Vietnam did, and his experiences at the hands of Union pillagers poison him to Reconstruction. Like Dave, Willie is also the defender of Southern womanhood, in this case a displaced Yankee abolitionist and a beautiful slave named Flower. He doesn't really do much to protect them, and he himself is saved from the worst of the Ku Klux Klan only because his best friend rides with them, but the thought is there. But *White Doves* also suffers from the same malaise which infects the Robicheaux books. Willie, like Dave, is a moral absolutist, who goes around righting tiny wrongs while accepting more serious ones as being beyond his remit. So the worst character, the slave-driver turned Confederate officer, turned Klansman, Rufus Atkins, simply drifts out of the book toward what we are assured was a bad fate. And the best, Willie's friend Robert Perry, is a Klansman separated from the rest only by altruism. He becomes a judge. This is particularly annoying in a book which suffers from Fried Green Tomato Syndrome, that is, a presence of characters with modern day sensibilities whom nobody finds out of place in the mid-19th century. Abigail, the Yankee woman, even puts down Rufus with a particularly nasty reference to his 'gene pool', which makes her a landmark genetic researcher as well. In the end, however, Rufus reminds us more of Simon Legree, and this is Burke's *Uncle Tom's Cabin.* Lincoln told Louisa Mae Alcott her book started the Civil War. Burke's simply revels in its aftermath.

Michael Carlson

No Second Chance
Harlan Coben
Orion, £12.99, 0752852566

It's a brave move for any writer to turn their back on a long-running character, especially one that's as popular as Myron Bolitar. But with this tough new thriller, Coben proves that he's more than up to the task of delivering a fine stand-alone novel. *No Second Chance* gives us the story of Marc Seidman, a doctor who is nearly killed during a break-in at his home. The consequences are terrible – his wife is killed and his six-month-old daughter Tara is abducted. But when the inevitable ransom demand is issued, the money drop goes horribly wrong and the kidnappers vanish. Eighteen months later, he receives a second ransom note offering him another chance. Is his daughter still alive? Who took her and why? The chase for answers – and his daughter – is on. All the characters are skllfully introduced and go on to develop in realistic and convincing ways. The plot is just as multi-layered as in Coben's previous books, the author's trademark fast-paced prose and short, sharp chapters making for a swift and satisfying read. If the ending fails to convince totally, then that's a small flaw in an otherwise very enjoyable book.

Mark Campbell

Lost Light
Michael Connelly
Orion, £17.99, 0752856561
A real return to form for Connelly, and a welcome return to action for Harry Bosch. When Bosch left the LAPD, he took a murder file with him – the victim being a film production assistant killed four years earlier during a multimillion dollar robbery on a movie set. Post 9/11, the LAPD thinks that the money was used to fund a terrorist training camp. Because it's such a high-profile case, the victims are lost in the media furore, and when it seems that the killer will be released to help the FBI find the terrorists, Bosch finds himself in conflict with both his ex-colleagues on the LAPD and the FBI. *Lost Light* is a gripping, intense novel; Bosch is a complex but very human character and *Lost Light* will cement Connelly's reputation.

Matt Levy

And another view...
Harry Bosch is back in the follow up to *City of Bones.* Now retired from the LAPD, he's a little quieter, a little less secure than he used to be. He's got a Hollywood district Private Investigator's licence, but he spends too much time learning to play the saxophone to make much use of it. But a chance meeting with an old colleague prompts him to look into an old murder case, that of Angella Benton, strangled on her front doorstep on her 24th birthday. The perpetrator of that – and a linked robbery heist – was never found. But Bosch thinks he might have a clue, and soon the FBI are leaning on him to drop his investigations – which must mean he's on the right track. Old faces from previous Bosch stories reappear here, but the mix gets a new twist with a revelatory first-person narrative opening up Bosch's thoughts like never before. Bosch's (and Connelly's) love of jazz shines through the text and LA is as convincingly described as ever. The plot might not be as smooth as other Bosch outings, but there's no disputing that Connelly has the knack of keeping you reading right up to the surprise ending.

Mark Campbell

The Last Detective
Robert Crais
Orion, £12.99, 0752851993
This is the first Elvis Cole novel since the remarkable *LA Requiem,* which was actually more about Elvis' partner Joe Pike. Crais has since delivered a couple of best-selling

suspense novels, and although he's now returned to his favourite private eye, in which each book he moves Elvis further from the low-key bounds of the hardboiled genre and more and more into the high-powered pages of suspense. As if to metaphorically complete the merging of styles, Carol Starkey, the former bomb-squad detective from *Demolition Angel* appears as the main investigator when the son of Lucy Chenier, Elvis' long-time girlfriend, is kidnapped – by someone who seems to be getting revenge for whatever Elvis did in Vietnam. Lucy's high-powered Louisiana hubby Richard appears on scene to point out the obvious: that ever since she met Cole, she and her son have been the targets of an inordinate amount of violence. And he's right! This is the fate of supporting players everywhere. It's also another sign of the changing nature of Crais' work: his Louisiana side, with its gothic darkness, is giving way to the Hollywood side, with the bright sunshine of LA the dominant aesthetic factor. There's still room for shadows. Joe Pike has not yet recovered fully from the wounds he received in *Requiem,* and Elvis' Vietnam experience is not something he'd wish to relive. In fact, there is a section when Elvis talks with the family of one of his dead Vietnam buddies that is as good a piece of writing as Crais has ever done. The story functions precisely, aided by multiple points of view for the narration. This helps convey a filmic quality, beyond the usual blockbuster rush to resolution suspense novels often tend to feature. Suspense is usually resolved by action, however, and Crais writes action slickly. Even though I figured out what was going on as early as page 73, I kept expecting to be faked out, to suffer twists that would prove me wrong. Crais supplied the twists, but I was still right. Not that I didn't keep reading, and admiring, how we got there. Sure there's a finish with a role that the next Haley Osmond will relish, but that's LA, and LA is Elvis territory.

Michael Carlson

The Devil's Handshake

Murray Davies

Macmillan, £16.99, 0333908430

For many, Hitler ranks amongst the greatest criminals in history. Ironic then that *The Devil's Handshake* centers upon a planned crime against the Führer and the efforts of a German detective, Jager, to unmask the British assassin parachuted into wartime Germany. Davies skillfully incorporates real events and people to create an unusual crime novel set against the greater back drop of World War Two. Opening atmospherically in Blitz-era London, the novel follows the preparation for the operation as agent Robin Lusty undergoes training for his dangerous role as an undercover killer. Behind the scenes machinations are exposed as political wheels turn both for and against the mission's success. The book is filled with characters such as Winston Churchill, Martin Bormann and Eva Braun and it is to Davies' credit that he succeeds in bringing them into three dimensional and credible life. *The Devil's Handshake* works well as a war thriller and a crime work, often highlighting the tensions between the German criminal police and the all-pervading Gestapo as a professional detective works to solve the case under the terrifying gaze of the Nazi party. Davies also succeeds in creating a portrait of a Germany increasingly riven with tensions as the war on the Russian front collapses and dissent, however secret, is growing at home. His evocation of landscapes and history are memorable and vivid and his attention to detail renews interest in a subject matter, which could in the wrong hands fall into the realms of parody. We are spared B-movie scenes of Nazi guards shouting "Schnell, schnell!" and are given a more sensitive and involving treatment of the suffering of the German people in World War Two.

Vic Buckner

The Serpent in the Garden

Janet Gleeson

Bantam Press, £12.99, 0593050908

A murderous tale of mystery and intrigue set in 18th century London by the ingenious Gleeson, author of *The Grenadillo Box*. The renowned artist Joshua Pope Esq has been hired to paint a wedding portrait of the recently widowed landowner, Herbert Bentnick, and his bride-to-be, Elinor Mercier, at their stately manor house in Richmond. Astley House has become testament to Elinor Mercier's enthusiasm for exotic horticulture and her expertise in the cultivation of pineapples. These curious fruits have just begun to appear in Georgian England and the country has gone wild for the new extravagant and fashionable delicacy. Delicately transported from the West Indies, the plants – requiring precise temperature, light and moisture control – have been planted in a specially constructed pinery. As Joshua progresses with the painting, and final preparations for the wedding are taking place, a ghastly discovery is made which will threaten all their comfortable lives: a body is found in the pinery. The murdered man is the first link in a chain of events which will dredge up secrets thought safely buried in the past. Can Joshua Pope solve this dormant mystery? And more pressingly, as his investigation progresses, can he stay alive long enough to finally reveal the truth? Gleeson proves she is no one-trick pony with this clever concoction.

Eve Tan Gee

Felaheen

Jon Courtenay Grimwood

Simon & Schuster, £12.99, 0743461177

Grimwood continues to be one of the most stylish and innovative writers at work today, throwing off remarkable literary conceits with true panache. Ashraf Bey has been many things since arriving in El Iskandryia from Seattle: detective, diplomat and killer. One thing he hasn't been, as yet, is a son to Moncef, Emir of Tunis – the father he has still to meet. Of course, Raf doesn't believe the

Emir is his father anyway. And now it may be too late to find out, since the rumours that don't have Moncef escaping assassination have him hovering on the edge of death. And Raf has his own part in an unfolding political crisis that began decades earlier with US anti-globalisation riots and the Emir's refusal to ratify the 2005 UN Accord on Biotechnology. Grimwood on coruscating form.

King of Torts

John Grisham

Century, £16.99, 0712670599

Grisham is going to greater and greater lengths to demonstrate how one bad barrel can spoil any one good legal apple. This time it's over-worked and under-paid public defender Clay Carter who's about to discover the worm inside. The key words, of course, are underpaid, because Grisham remains enough of a lawyer himself to remember poverty is the one sin no lawyer can afford. Clay has a Southern nouveau-belle girlfriend who listens to her parents when they prove Clay is a ne'er do well, so presumably Grisham is giving Clay motivation to accept the offer to become a tort lawyer, representing victims of a faulty drug, when a mysterious stranger makes him the kind of offer anyone other than a lawyer would see offers some problems if one accepts. Soon, Clay is the new 'King of Torts', bringing settlements in that make him worth millions, and discovering the pleasures of money in best legal fashion: which means more and more expensive toys. Because, like the ethics professor lawyer in *The Summons*, Clay appears to be functionally impotent. He never has sex with his girlfriend, and then he picks up a trophy model, with whom his contact appears limited to exchanging credit card details, not flesh. And of course, the business goes wrong, and, shock horror! Clay discovers he's been used, and much of what he has done is shock horror! illegal, not to mention unethical and certainly, for those of us not lawyers, immoral. So how is it resolved? Well, Clay skates on the crimes, his friends give him a few million to tide him over outside the country, and he gets the plastic southern belle of his dreams, who's already divorced her husband of a few months. Clay is also the victim of a beating, making him literally, as well as figuratively impotent. I give his new relationship three months, and the money from his friends a year. Grisham's best-sellers are straight out of *Dynasty*, only with less depth. The world has caught up to them.

Michael Carlson

And another view...

Reviews for Grisham's latest have been mixed, with many reviewers disappointed that Grisham's ability to work up a thriller may have left him. But they miss the point, I feel. *The King of Torts* is not a thriller, it is a fable of modern America's love for litigation as a way of life; a love lit, fuelled and fanned by lawyers, but a love in which a greedy and gullible public is easily wooed. Grisham sets his novel in the rapacious world of tort litigation, in the churning waters which breed America's richest and most outrageous legal sharks. Lawyer Clay Carter is not one of these. A journeyman in the Office of the Public Defender, he is one day approached by the Mephistophelean Max Price and offered a tilt at unbounded wealth. Like Faust, Carter sells his soul to achieve his dream – and achieve it he does, initially: fame, a hundred million dollars and the world's most beautiful mistress. But in an American take on the old Faustian legend, money does not buy what Clay wants. He is wakened from his dream into a waking nightmare. It's not a thriller, it's modern life – and that's much more scary.

Russell James

Blood is the Sky

Steve Hamilton

Orion, £12.99, 0752852760

Michigan, October. Alex McKnight is rebuilding one of his cabins with friend Vinne LeBlanc when LeBlanc is called to an emergency – his brother, Tom, has not returned from hunting and is four days overdue. Alex and Vinnie decide to retrace the hunt party's steps, travelling as far as the Ontario roads will allow. When they arrive at the outpost they are told that the hunters have already left to return to Michigan. But something's wrong. Vinnie and Alex – aided by a Cree Indian and his grandfather – fly to the outpost, only to find a terrible secret. Alex and Vinnie are miles from home with no food and equipment – but someone doesn't want them to get home alive. Superb visualization of Canadian countryside with original characterization make this one to watch.

Matt Levy

Death's Jest-Book

Reginald Hill

HarperCollins, £6.99, 0007123442

In recent years and recent novels Reginald Hill has abandoned the comforting confines of the conventional police procedural and attempted something far more ambitious in his fiction. His books have become vast, sprawling narratives in which several plots criss-cross and interweave and a small army of recurring characters reveals its all too flawed humanity. *Death's Jest-Book* is no exception. Franny Roote, the joker in the pack of previous novels, has returned to plague DCI Pascoe with a series of letters in which he appears again to be playing his own peculiar mind-games. Is he hinting at crimes committed that he believes Pascoe is too stupid to pin on him? DC Hat Bowler has returned to work after his violent confrontation with the serial killer, the Wordman, in *Dialogues of the Dead,* but the case still has surprises to spring. And, as the threads of three different plots converge, even the formidable figure of the Fat Man, DS Andy Dalziel, finds the realities of death and fate difficult to confront. Hill has often been hailed as one of Britain's best crime novelists. As this extraordinary, brilliantly written tour de force demonstrates, he's

better described just as one of Britain's best novelists.

Nick Rennison

Point of Impact

Stephen Hunter

Arrow, £6.99, 0099453452

It's about time this, the first of the Bob Lee Swagger novels to be written before *Dirty White Boys* and *Black Light,* appeared in paperback, so kudos to Arrow for bringing it back into print. The Swagger saga, particularly the two novels starring Bob Lee's father Earl, are first and foremost action books, and in *Point of Impact* Bob Lee probably comes the closest to his father's characterisation. There isn't the depth of the two books which followed, particularly *Black Light,* which I consider Hunter's best, but there is a hell of a set-up, where Bob Lee finds himself turned into the mother of all Lee Harvey Oswalds. Hunter's books are also about weapons, and this obsession with hardware is also a strength, because the reader soon realises that Hunter's protagonist is just another piece of finely crafted hardware himself. Bob Lee proves over and over that no amount of technology, of psy-op plannings, of legal or governmental fixing can overcome one of America's good ol' boy natural born killers. This is, in a strange way, reassuring, because it's odd how in Hunter's books there is so much faith in America and so much evidence that its institutions are corrupt to the core. Or the corps, in Bob Lee's case. The story revolves around loyalty, and trust, and basically if you put yours in Swagger, you won't go wrong. The same advice might be given readers, as well.

Michael Carlson

A Cold Heart

Jonathan Kellerman

Headline, £12.99, 0747267022

Kellerman's form has been fitful of late, but this is top-drawer stuff. Juliet Kipper, a gifted painter, is strangled in the LA gallery where her first solo show has opened to critical acclaim, and Milo Sturgis takes on the murder investigation as a favour to an old friend. He consults Alex Delaware, who, researching parallels with other deaths, looks for artists killed when on the verge of a breakthrough or comeback. And he finds two others. A few weeks earlier, blues player Edgar Michael 'Baby Boy' Lee was stabbed just after finishing his set at The Snakepit. The investigation points to a gruesome, sadistic pattern of death taking Milo and Alex into terrible danger. Kellerman's experience as psychologist adds layers of verisimilitude to this tautly written thriller.

Judith Gray

John le Carré: The Spy Who Became a Writer

NordPark, 11 Euros, 3935421125

Mainly in German of course. But, if you are a le Carré fan or student, hear me out. After all, most le Carré studies came out in the 1980s and do not take into account his change in direction in the post-Cold War period. Still less are there publications with the kind of dazzling bibliography that is included here. This is the second in a useful series of monographs from NordPark (the first featured German writer Michael Preute). It consists of a 40-odd page critical portrait of the writer in question by Hindersmann, along with a thorough (50 page) bibliography using British, American and German sources from German archivist and bibliographer Przybilka. Not too many surprises in Hindersmann's dissertation, judging by the key points laid out in English in two pages at the rear of the book. Przybilka's bibliography is however something else. Along with the expected list of le Carré's books in both their British and German editions, there are lists of other le Carré writings: newspaper articles, prefaces from books, etc, covering 1964 to date (early 2002), along with key interviews from 1977 onwards. There are also reviews of le Carré books listed by title. And backing all that up, extensive lists of the reference books, biographies and critical works, magazine and newspaper articles that cover le Carré and the spy novel in its many forms. Truly impressive.

Bob Cornwell

(Available from Buchandlung Missing Link, Zweigniederlassung Bonn, Thomas Przybilka, Buchstrasse 14, D-53113 Bonn, Germany. Missing Link accepts both Visa and MasterCard.)

Circles & Squares

John Malcolm

Allison & Busby, £17.99, 074900584X

As I write this, a major Ben Nicholson exhibition is opening in St Ives, and, by coincidence, Ben and his father, Sir William, are the artists at the heart of this latest Tim Simpson mystery. Simpson is the former rugby player/art dealer who is constantly getting into scrapes with the law, which is good because it leaves him time to meet with his copper friend Nobby at a café near Victoria (the author, it should be noted, lives in Sussex) and indulge in a breakfast "incorporating two fried eggs, rashers of bacon, tomato, mushrooms, sausages, fried bread, black pudding if you want it, baked beans and fried potatoes or American hash browns, all at a very reasonable price". Is this something the reader really needs to know? When the narrator sounds like a waitress reciting a menu, it's no surprise that the characters sound like they're reading pages of art history off Encarta to each other. That's when they're not saying things like "what ho", "my humble doorstep" and "forsooth". That must've been some tough rugby club Tim played on. It's as if the cast of a Sherlock Holmes story had wandered into an Agatha Christie radio play to take quick 'shuftis' at each other. But then, when Nobby is joined by characters named Dorkie, Alpie, Geoffrey, Gerry, Jimmie and Murray Finch-Hatton, all that's missing is Sleepy, Dopey, Grumpy and, of course, Cosy. So if that sort of cosy is your sort of thing, this may be your sort of thing. My advice, if you're keen on either of the Nicholsons, is make the drive to Cornwall, and leave the seven dwarves to their own devices.

Michael Carlson

The Runner
Peter May
Hodder & Stoughton, £18.99, 0340823739
Peter May's very readable Chinese series continues with detective Li Yan back in Beijing accompanied by, although not legally living with, his pregnant American fiancée Margaret Campbell. Usefully, she's a pathologist – frowned upon by the Chinese authorities but dragged into Li's latest case when it appears to concern the highly sophisticated doping of top Chinese athletes. Campbell's skills are needed for the same reason Li's are: Olympic athletes are dying – and their deaths are being made to look accidental. The story tracks a somewhat predictable course towards the perpetrator, but far more interestingly gives an absorbing and well informed account of Beijing life today and the inside workings of the Chinese police. While the case puzzles the Chinese, they find the deaths less strange than Li's determination to wed a foreigner. The embattled couple face implacable opposition while at the same time they raise the ire of highly placed – and perhaps closely placed? – Chinese villains. Doping, Triads, high-level corruption and a heroine eight months pregnant. What more could you ask? Only an imminent wedding, with the hostile parents-in-law meeting for the first time. Far from a *dim sum,* this fare turns out quite piquant.

Russell James

A Feast of Carrion
Keith McCarthy
Constable, £16.99, 1841196193
A whodunit in the classical mould mixes the story of a man coping with the scars of his past and the wounds of the present, and a tentative love story; McCarthy handles his material with real brio. St Benjamin's Museum of Pathology is the greatest of its kind. Any death occurring within its walls would create far-reaching ripples in the academic world, but the death of Nikki Exner is far from just any death. Raped, then hung, drawn and quartered, her grotesque demise sickened everyone. Chief Inspector Castle has problems of his own and isn't interested in the investigation, but his deputy, Inspector Beverley Wharton, doesn't mind. She knows that this is going to do her nothing but good, and when she discovers that Tim Bilroth, known rapist and drug addict, is on the museum staff, she knows he is her murderer. Bilroth is arrested and when he commits suicide in custody, his guilt seems certain. However, Helen Flemming, a solicitor with good reason to dislike Wharton, suspects she is wrong. McCarthy has been practising pathology since 1985. He is currently a

consultant histopathologist in Gloucestershire, but this doesn't suggest (as it might) that this is a case of 'good research, shame about the writing'; McCarthy cuts it in that area too.

Ingrid Yornstrand

Clean Cut

Theresa Monsour

Time Warner, £16.99, 0316861790

With the crime genre groaning at the seams with authors, it's hard to imagine there's much room left for many new additions to the fold. But there is, and her name is Theresa Monsour. *Clean Cut* is a debut novel that is as assured as it is powerful and looks destined to kickstart Monsour to the pantheon of crime writers. Her heroine is one Paris Murphy, an Irish-Lebanese detective, who, together with her partner Gabe Nash, is on the hunt for a rather unpleasant serial killer who's not adverse to a spot of necrophilia and depilation. But things turn even nastier when the killer starts hunting her. This is a very gripping debut. There are strong echoes of Michael Connelly in the jazz references and travelogue-like details, and both share the same desire to tell as exciting a story as possible. Monsour wins out in the gore stakes though, with more gruesome images than Connelly ever allows. Be warned – there are vivid descriptions of the killer at work which are definitely not for the faint-hearted. Paris' own reactions to the rapes add a deeper layer of complexity to the plot and shows that Monsour is unafraid to tackle contentious issues. A bona fide page-turner.

Mark Campbell

Weaving Shadows

Margaret Murphy

Hodder & Stoughton, £18.99, 0340820543

A woman beaten to death with a hammer. A man shot in cold blood. A crooked cop taking backhanders: but barrister Clara Pascal thinks she is taking on a simple child custody case. Traumatised by her own experiences as a kidnap victim, Clara works to keep the shadows of the past from affecting her friends, family and work. But the dreams don't get any easier and the past won't go away. Then Clara finds herself thrown back into a crime investigation she wants nothing to do with. Her client is a convicted killer, one who stalks and photographs young women – so why does Clara believe that he's innocent? Risking everything, Clara sets out to prove that the past has no hold on the future – while a killer comes ever closer to making her the next victim. Murphy's excellent books are all concerned with the psychology of both the violent criminal and the victim of crime, and the new book will add lustre to her reputation.

Judith Gray

Back Story

Robert B Parker

John Murray, £17.99, 0719562910

Although this is one of the strongest Spenser novels in recent years, perhaps Parker called it *Back Story* because so much of it is so familiar. Spenser's surrogate son, Paul, shows up with an actress friend who wants Spenser to investigate her mother's death, as an innocent bystander when a radical group robbed a bank, some 30 years earlier. Which is, coincidentally, just about the time Spenser started detecting around Boston, and maybe it's because I'm old enough to remember those days, but the radical gang could've been characters right out of George Higgins' *Friends of Eddie Coyle.* Time, the passage thereof, is an increasingly sensitive subject for the world's most sensitive tough guy.

Pearl, the Wonder Dog, has died offstage since the last Spenser novel, sparing the audience many tears, but her replacement, Pearl II, is every bit as cute, so cute in fact I'm surprised Spenser doesn't get another dog called Knit One to go with her. Of course, in Boston, it's detectives who age in dog years, not dogs. Of course, the death of an innocent bystander turns out to be anything but, and as the investigation delves deeper into the past more and more familiar scenes pop up, not least when hitman Vinnie Morris and a couple of local gangstas are recruited to protect Spenser's fair queen, Susan. She's so used to this by now that when someone says her apartment has a homey feel, she thinks of hooded sweatshirts and automatic weapons. There's even a guest appearance by Paradise, Mass., chief of police Jesse Stone, who manages to refrain from referring either Spenser or Hawk to a psychotherapist. The story peters out into a resumption of the status quo, as so many Spenser books have done recently. Could Parker's soft-centred hardboiled hero be turning cosy on us after all these years?

Michael Carlson

Gunman's Rhapsody

Robert B Parker

Berkeley (USA), $7.99, 0425182894

In *Potshot*, Parker had Spenser assemble his own Magnificent Seven, to do gun battle with a band of renegades led by The Preacher. It was fun in a tongue-in-cheek kind of way, but the idea of Spenser as Western hero must have been lodged in Parker's mind, because *Gunman's Rhapsody* is the story of Wyatt Earp and the Gunfight at the OK Corral. This is not necessarily the key Western myth in American culture, but it is, along with the stories of Jesse James and Billy the Kid, the one which has been adapted most often. The Earp story is many-faceted: his relations with his brothers, and his women; the odd pairing with Doc Holliday; the cast of villains, ranging from the rustling Clantons to the classics-quoting gunman Johnny Ringo, and not least, the politics of Tombstone, the aptly named silver-mine boom town. Earp is eminently adaptable, just think of the films. He's been a sleazy politician (Frank Perry's *Doc*), a reluctant civiliser (John Ford's *My Darling Clementine*), a morally ambiguous figure bent on revenge (John Sturges' *Hour of the Gun)* and a santicmonius bore (Lawrence Kasdan's *Wyatt Earp*). He's been played by everyone from Walter Huston to Kurt Russell. Mountains of non-fiction books have argued whether he was hero or villain, valiant gunman or self-promoting spin-doctor. So what approach does Parker take? Simple. Earp becomes Spenser, a century early. When you think about it, it makes sense. What is Hawk if not a black, non-consumptive, Doc Holliday? If you saw Dana Delany as Josie Marcus in *Tombstone*, as Parker surely did, you'd realise she's a pre-Freudian Susan Silverman. What makes it work, as ever with Parker, is his skill with dialogue; and as usual Earp/Spenser gets most of the last words (though he seems to have a fond spot for Virgil Earp, whose voice sounds suspiciously like Sam Elliott's, who played Virg in the aforementioned *Tombstone*). This is the story of gangs fighting for domination in a sort of urban environment; and it's also a story of revenge and honour. Parker gives us as good an explanation of Ringo's bizarre death as we're likely to get. You get the sense Wyatt and Spenser might have been happy to compare notes. But I can't see Wyatt copying down the Boston tough-guy's recipes.

Michael Carlson

Samaritan

Richard Price

Bloomsbury, £12.99, 0747562245

Ray Mitchell is a storyteller with a mission. He returns, sacked from his Hollywood screenwriting job, to teach English to the 'thug-life kids' in the wastelands of his hometown in New Jersey. His evangelical desire to 'give something back' to the housing projects that formed him is returned by an act of violence that results in Ray fighting for his life in a hospital bed. Mute with self-loathing he refuses to give up his attacker. Only childhood friend turned cop, Nerese Ammons, can pick at Ray's wounds to uncover the truth. Richard Price, the Tolstoy of the urban thriller and New York's anti-Tom Wolfe, punctuates his Hollywood screenwriting career once more with a triumphant follow-up to *Clockers* and *Freedomland*. Turning a riveting whodunit into a social document, he keeps intact the thriller element amongst the personal drama and uses his unmatchable ear for street dialogue to fine-tune the truth of everyday language. Turning on their head the preconceived stereotypes of the ghetto, he humanises the inhabitants of a world shaped by the jailyard chic of rap videos, treading water to survive, and invites us to spend some time 'daytripping in the house of pain'. Give this man an Oscar.

Mike Paterson

Winter's End

John Rickards

Michael Joseph, £10.00, 0718145836

Winter's End is a grim and compelling psychological thriller which marks Rickards out as a key new voice in crime thriller fiction. Ex-FBI agent turned private investigator, Rourke knows about the twisted minds of murderers. If anyone can get inside the head of a tricky suspect, he can. But the killer in *Winter's End* is playing a clever game and it is imperative that Rourke plays to win. How does he know so much about the local area? Has he been there before? Strange, in that case, since no one recognises him. And how does he know so much about Rourke: his history in the FBI; the death of his parents? Debut novels often have a tentative feel: not so here. Rickards delivers the good like an old hand.

Ralph Travis

Two by Ripley

Angel enthusiasts know what to expect form

the reliable Ripley, and these two deliver the usual sharp-edged antics.

Angel on the Inside

Mike Ripley

Constable Robinson, £16.99, 1841196681

So why is Angel trying to break into a prison? The trouble starts when Angel's wife Amy's ex-husband is re-arrested, having been released from prison only a month before. And some very seedy characters start taking a close interest in what the ex-husband was doing in between his release from prison and subsequent re-arrest for stalking Amy – but Amy's not talking. It's up to Angel to find out why his wife is being so reticent and why another mystery person is so fascinated by the ex's movements – and the only way to do that is to discover what was going on in prison prior to his release. So Angel has to figure out how to break in; he doesn't know yet how he'll do it, only that it's going to be just like *The Great Escape* – only in reverse...

Angel Underground

Mike Ripley

Constable Robinson, £6.99, 184119669X

Out of the blue, Angel is contacted by his mother who is living a semi-bohemian life in darkest Suffolk. She is concerned about one of her neighbours who has decided to fund a private archaeological dig on his own farmland, convinced he will find the remains from Queen Boudica's royal mint. There have been sinister accidents on site and several diggers have been attacked, so the Angel decides he must infiltrate the dig – only to discover it has already been infiltrated by individuals intent on finding a grave far more recent than the Iron Age.

Eve Tan Gee

Dissolution

C J Sansom

Pan, £10.99, 1405005572

A highly promising first novel which is already garnering advance praise from the likes of P D James, this is a historical crime novel that redefines the genre. 1537, England. The Dissolution of the Monasteries is under way. Henry VIII has proclaimed himself Supreme Head of the Church. The country is waking up to savage new laws, rigged trials and the greatest network of informers it has ever seen. Under the orders of Thomas Cromwell, a team of commissioners is sent throughout the country to investigate the monasteries. There can only be one outcome: the monasteries are to be dissolved. But on the Sussex coast, at the monastery of Scarnsea, events have spiralled out of control. Cromwell's commissioner, Robin Singleton, has been found dead, his head severed from his body. His horrific murder is accompanied by equally sinister acts of sacrilege – a black cockerel sacrificed on the church altar, and the disappearance of Scarnsea's Great Relic. Matthew Shardlake, lawyer and long-time supporter of reform, has been sent by Cromwell into this atmosphere of treachery and death, accompanied by his loyal assistant Mark. His duty is to uncover the truth behind the dark happenings at Scarnsea. Shardlake's investigation soon forces him to question everything that he hears, and everything that he intrinsically believes... Historical details seamlessly wedded to a powerful narrative gift.

Ingrid Yornstrand

Traitor's Kiss

Gerald Seymour

Bantam, £12.99, 0593050916

When I call this a classic adventure thriller I

give it nothing but awed praise. It begins at MI6's Russia Desk; much of the action is in the Russian enclave of Kaliningrad; but this is as exciting a thriller as it is possible to write. In what remains of the Russian navy a man has passed information to the British since 1998. Now his cover is blown. He appeals to the British to get him out. Kaliningrad is a historical anomaly, a strip of land in western Europe, part of the old Soviet Union, an important naval base, heavily defended and almost impossible to enter. Or exit. Today's MI6 would leave him to his fate – but one charismatic veteran is allowed to lead a small team on a safe, deniable retrieval exercise. You see? It *is* a classic adventure thriller – but superbly done. The team, of course, comprises SAS throw-outs, one of whom is plucked from jail. There's a love interest. And to 'help' comes one of the new breed of MI6 men, opposed to the old-fashioned fieldcraft of dead letter drops and human intelligence. The tension builds, the pace becomes unstoppable, and the ending will keep you up at night.

Russell James

Clea's Moon

Edward Wright

Orion, £10.99, 0752852906

Washed up B-movie cowboy actor John Ray Horn is out collecting debts for his Indian co-star, Joseph Mad Crow (great name), when an old friend turns up with some incriminating photos discovered in his late father's possessions. To Horn's dismay, one of them features his stepdaughter Clea. And he's even more shocked a few days later when he finds his friend murdered and his stepdaughter missing. Using only the photos as clues, Horn begins to track her down, but it's a journey fraught with danger... Set against a pulsating 1940s Los Angeles, this is an atmospheric and compelling novel with a commendably original double-act at its centre – the idea of unemployed cowboy film stars becoming detectives is charming, and Horn and Crow prove to be a great team. Like James Ellroy's *LA Confidential*, Wright's story centres on the sleazier side of Hollywood, be it from the moneyed heights of the Hollywood Hills to the desperation of Gower Gulch, a place where budding cowboy actors tout for business. Rich with the sights, sounds and smells of this capital of film noir, *Clea's Moon* is an amazing debut novel. And unlike their films, the literary adventures of this B-movie team will surely run and run.

Mark Campbell